Debate

As the audience burst into applause, Holly jumped up and gave Greg an excited hug. They had won! The debate was theirs and so was third place in the whole tournament!

Suddenly someone grabbed her and lifted her into the air. "What . . . ?" she gasped.

"Holly, you were great!" Zachary McGraw exclaimed.

"What are you — "

He swung her through the air.

"Let me down!" she cried. "Let me go!"

Bart and Diana were staring at Holly from twenty feet away. Bart's eyes glared coldly at her. Before Holly could go to them or even call out, they turned and hurried from the auditorium.

Holly sank down onto the floor, and the tears started to spill from her eyes.

COUPLES

TAKE ME BACK

M.E. Cooper

SCHOLASTIC INC.
New York Toronto London Auckland Sydney

ISBN 0-590-41264-7

12 11 10 9 8 7 6 5 4 3 2 1   8 9/8 0 1 2 3/9

Printed in the U.S.A.   01

First Scholastic printing, February 1988

TAKE ME BACK

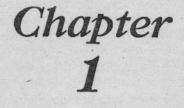

Chapter 1

"Hey, Holly! Heads up!"

Holly Daniels looked up. A huge wet snowball was coming straight at her. She dodged to one side and smiled triumphantly as the snowball sailed past her, then gasped as she watched it catch Jonathan Preston on the side of the head. Jonathan whirled around.

"Whoever did that is going to get buried in a snowdrift!" he yelped. "Which one of you tuna heads is responsible?"

Matt Jacobs, Jonathan's best friend, raised both hands over his head. "I surrender," he began. "It was all — " Jonathan tossed a handful of snow in his face, and Matt sputtered to a halt.

Kennedy High School was back in session after two snow days, and everyone had energy to burn. Holly looked around the quad where her friends — the crowd — always met. On the other side, a gang of sophomores was playing "keep away"

1

with hard-packed snowballs. Nearby, some juniors were building an enormous snowman, so tall that the girl working on its face had to sit on a friend's shoulders to reach. Every time she leaned forward to try and put the eyes on, her friend took a step backward to keep his balance. The third time, she leaned so far forward that he lost his footing. They both toppled into the deep snow and sat up laughing.

Pamela Green, a gifted artist in the senior class, was kneeling at the base of a leafless cherry tree, sculpting the snow into the shape of a dog. Holly bent down to look it over.

"What is it?" she asked. "A German shepherd?"

Pamela laughed and brushed her hair away from her eyes. "No, it's a husky," she said. "All this snow reminded me of Alaska — and then I started thinking about sled dogs. I wanted to sculpt a husky looking off into the distance — maybe at a glacier — but I can't quite get the head at the right angle."

Holly gazed around at the quad with its thick, gleaming blanket of snow. It really did look like a scene in the Far North.

"Hey, that's it!" Pamela exclaimed, adding more snow. "Don't move."

Holly followed orders, but she found it hard to stay still. She had never modeled for a statue before — especially not one of a dog. Besides, she really needed to blow off some steam. For her, the two snow days had not been much of a vacation. She had needed them to study for the upcoming debate tournament at the University of Virginia. This was the first year the debate team from Kennedy had been invited to compete. It was quite an honor, or so everyone said. Holly wasn't so sure. To her, it felt like just one more thing to worry about. She didn't even *like* debating that much. Every time her turn came to stand up and present an argument, her stomach tied itself up into knots. Once she had tried explaining to her best friend, Diana Einerson, how nervous it made her.

"Then why do it?" Diana had asked in her most sensible voice.

"I need some more extracurricular activities on my record," she replied, blushing. "I thought debating would look good on my college applications." What Holly didn't say, but what they both knew, was that she desperately wanted to get into the premed program at the University of Montana. Bart, Holly's boyfriend and Diana's brother, was in the middle of his freshman year there, and Holly was hoping she would be able to join him next year.

"But why debating?" Diana said after a pause. "You want to be a doctor, not a lawyer."

Holly shook her head. "I don't really know. I saw the notice and went to the first meeting, that's all. And once I signed up, I couldn't let myself quit. I never expected to make the team, though," she added. "Now I wish I hadn't."

Despite her feelings, the team was having a very good year. A lot of the credit belonged to her teammate, Greg Montgomery. Greg was a born debater, who always found just the right words he needed to make his argument convincing. But Holly's long hours in the library, researching the

3

assigned topics, contributed quite a bit, too. Sometimes she wished that she could just do the research and let Greg do all the talking!

Holly looked around, forgetting Pamela's plea to stay still. Greg was standing a dozen feet away, talking quietly to his girlfriend, Katie. Katie's leg was in a cast from a recent skiing accident that cut short her career as a gymnast. A few weeks earlier, before the accident, Katie would have been dashing around, throwing snowballs at whoever was in range. Now, on crutches, practically all she could do was stand by and smile. It surprised Holly that Katie *was* able to smile. In her place, Holly thought, she probably would have been chewing her nails off in sheer frustration.

"There!" said Pamela, getting to her feet and brushing the loose snow off her hands. *"The Call of the Wild."*

"Hey, neat," Holly said. She studied the snow sculpture, which really did look like a sled dog.

Holly glanced over at Pamela, trying to imagine what it was like to have a special talent like that. Sometimes she envied creative people like Pamela, who could turn a pile of snow into a lifelike dog in just a few minutes. But Holly knew that one of her own strengths was her absolute determination to go into medicine. That desire had been part of her for almost all her life. As a little girl, Holly was always bandaging up scrapes for the boys in her old neighborhood. And then in junior high, as soon as she was old enough, Holly had signed up as a candy striper. Now she was working at the medical clinic of the Rose Hill Hospital after school. And of course, she was taking courses in biology and chemistry.

Holly had put in a lot of work at school and at the hospital because she wanted to become a doctor, but even so it seemed that her life had been a lot less complicated before she discovered love. Everything seemed simple at first — she fell in love with Bart and he fell in love with her. What could be easier? She smiled as she thought of those early days, when they had spent so much time together and had so much fun, though Bart seemed to flirt constantly with other girls. He claimed that it didn't mean anything, but it nearly tore them apart. With support from their friends, they had worked it out. Holly learned how important she was to him, and Bart learned how much all his flirting hurt her feelings. In some ways, they became closer after having worked out their problems together. But they also became aware of how much they could hurt each other.

"Oops, sorry!"

Holly nearly fell over into the snow as a girl ran into her at breakneck speed. Before she could recover her balance, she staggered again as a guy with a handful of snow ran into both of them.

"Sorry," he called to Holly as he laughingly tried to stuff the snow down the neck of the other girl's ski jacket. She shrieked, dodged past Holly, and ran across the quad with the guy right behind her.

Holly shook her head. It felt weird to have so many new faces around. She was used to knowing practically everybody at school, at least by sight, but things had changed. When the authorities decided to close nearby Stevenson High because of a decline in enrollment, Kennedy received one third of the Stevenson student body — almost a hundred students. They were just like any high school kids, but as a group, their arrival was making life at Kennedy more complicated. And one of them, in particular, had been making Holly's life *much* more complicated.

As if in response to her thoughts, Zachary McGraw walked by and caught her eye. She blushed and looked away. Holly rubbed the backs of her mittens across her cheeks and wished they didn't feel so hot. She liked the junior from Stevenson; he was very sweet, and he obviously liked her a lot. But there was hardly anything going on between them. They had talked a few times, and they were friends, but that was it — except for a brief kiss at the Valentine's Day Dance a week and a half ago.

And that kiss had been totally unexpected — almost accidental. Unlike most people at the dance, Holly hadn't signed up for a computer Valentine, where a computer would match you up with a compatible date. But she received a print-out anyway, that gave the time, place, and password for meeting her secret Valentine. Holly didn't know what to make of her computer date. She half thought it might be Bart — home to surprise her for Valentine's Day. But when Holly went to meet her date, she found herself wrapped up in the arms of Zachary McGraw. And her lonely evening without Bart turned into a surprisingly romantic one.

One single kiss. Was that so awful? Holly

didn't think so, but since then, she had been wishing that nothing had ever happened between her and Zack. She found herself worrying constantly that one of her friends had seen them. If Bart ever found out, it would be a disaster. He might be a flirt himself, but he was also a very jealous guy, and she loved him too much to want to see him hurt.

She was worrying over nothing, she reminded herself. No one had seen them kissing, and even if somebody had, so what? Who would be upset enough, or mean enough, to tell Bart? She shouldn't have let herself get into this crazy situation, but she knew she could get herself out of it without hurting anyone. She had plenty of time to let Zachary down gently before Bart came home for his spring break. Once she and Bart were together again, everything would be just the way it used to be.

She glanced around and smiled. The bunch of juniors had almost finished their big snowman. A multicolored ski hat and a striped scarf gave it a sporty look, and someone had placed a battered paperback of *The Scarlet Letter* in its stick arm. The Kennedy snowman was all ready for Mr. Barclay's sophomore English class.

One of the people admiring the snowman was Diana. Holly's smile broadened as she carefully molded a snowball and tossed it at her best friend. Diana gave a shriek of laughter, grabbed up a big handful of snow, and whirled around. Holly grinned and buried her face in her arm to block Diana's counterattack.

Nothing happened. Was Diana holding off,

waiting for Holly to lower her guard? She peeped cautiously over her arm, bracing herself for a faceful of snow. Diana wasn't there. Where was she? Sneaking around to attack her from behind? Holly lowered her arm and looked around in puzzlement.

Across the quad, she saw her friend about to enter the school building. It wasn't like Diana to walk away from a friendly snowball fight. She hadn't even said hello to her. Holly glanced at her watch — still five more minutes before class. Fighting off a growing sense of dismay, Holly hurried after her and caught up near their lockers.

"Hi," she said. "Isn't the snow terrific? I love it when it's still fluffy, before it all turns to slush."

Diana was too busy with her combination lock to answer.

"I tried calling you a couple of times this week," Holly continued, "to see if you wanted to come over. I guess you didn't get the messages."

"I've been very busy," Diana said, opening her locker. She turned sideways and reached in, turning her back on Holly.

"Um, me, too," said Holly. Her throat was tightening up, making it hard to speak. What was the matter with Diana? Had Holly done something wrong? She decided to change the subject. "The debating team's got a big invitational meet at UVA in a couple of weeks, so I've been hitting the library pretty steadily. I haven't even had a chance to think about my history project yet — are you working on yours already? Maybe you

8

can give me some ideas for it. That's one of the things I wanted to talk to you about, but I couldn't reach you."

"I was out at Danberry Stable a lot," Diana said. "Horses have to be taken care of, you know." She sounded as if it was all Holly's fault that she had to take care of her horse. "I spent a lot of time with Jeremy, too, if you must know."

"Oh, right." Something was *definitely* wrong. Diana had never acted this coldly to her before. Well, not since Holly's big falling out with Bart, which was practically a year ago. She had hardly seen or talked to Diana since the Valentine's Day Dance. Holly's heart fell. Had Diana, of all people, somehow found out about Zachary? It didn't seem possible. But it was the only explanation Holly could find for the way Diana was acting.

Diana pulled out the book she wanted, slammed the locker closed, and fastened the lock. Holly knew that in another moment, she would turn and walk away. She tugged nervously at the collar of her sweater. "I'm really glad that everyone's friends again — after Katie's accident, I mean," Holly said. "Aren't you? I mean, we've all known each other so long. It's terrible when people let a misunderstanding come between them like that."

"If it *is* a misunderstanding," Diana said in a grim voice.

"Oh, sure it is. I never really believed that it was anyone's *fault* that Katie had an accident, did you? It was just bad luck that Eric skied in front of her on his way over to help Roxanne. And after all, Katie herself said that she was the one who chose the hardest trail on the slope."

"Of course it wasn't Jonathan or Greg or Eric's fault." Diana had suddenly warmed up to Holly. "They were too busy playing up to that Roxanne Easton to *notice* what trail they were on."

Holly giggled. "She's awful, isn't she? But at least everybody found out what she was doing before she caused any more trouble. And I saw K.C. just now in the quad; she looked okay."

"Yeah, she's been pretty cheerful," Diana admitted. "And Greg seems to be helping her a lot."

She started down the hall. Holly fell into step beside her. Thank goodness whatever had been wrong with Diana was only short-lived.

"As for Roxanne, though," Diana continued, "she isn't finished making trouble, not by a long shot. Maybe we've patched up the feud in our crowd, but there's a bigger one brewing."

"There is?"

"Definitely," Diana said. "Roxanne's been telling all the kids from Stevenson that we're going out of our way to make things tough for them. They're believing her, too. Why not? It *is* tough moving to a new school. All she's doing is giving them somebody to blame for their problems: us."

"Nobody'll listen to her," Holly said. "They've known her longer than we have. They must have figured out what she's like by now."

"Well, they *are* listening," Diana insisted. "And they're starting to be suspicious of everything we do. If something isn't done soon, Kennedy is going to be split into two factions."

10

"Come on, Diana, you're exaggerating," said Holly. "I haven't noticed that kind of hostility from the Stevenson bunch. And anyway, what Roxanne is saying is obviously off base. Everybody's tried hard to make the kids from Stevenson feel welcome at Kennedy."

Diana stopped in her tracks and stared at Holly with narrowed eyes. "Yeah?" she said. "Well, maybe some of us have been trying a little *too* hard to make them feel welcome!"

Holly froze. There was no way to misunderstand what Diana had just said. Impossible as it seemed, Diana had somehow found out about Zachary. Had someone seen them kissing at the dance? Holly's heart sank. She longed to ask Diana what she knew, to try to explain, but she didn't dare. Diana might have been her best friend for a year, but she had been Bart's little sister all her life. There wasn't any question where her loyalties lay.

Diana's face tightened, as if Holly's reaction had confirmed all her suspicions. "There's something else you ought to know," she said icily. "Bart called the day before yesterday. He'll be finishing his exams early, so he's coming here for spring break sooner than he thought. He asked me not to tell you because he wanted it to be a surprise. But I thought you deserved a warning. There have been enough surprises around here already."

She turned and stalked away without waiting for a response. That was just as well. Holly was too stunned to respond. Bart was coming home? She wanted to feel glad, but the sick feeling in her

11

stomach wouldn't let her. She had to talk to Zack right away. She had to tell him that she couldn't have anything more to do with him. He would be very hurt, she knew, but what else could she do? Unless she acted quickly, she was going to lose both her best friend and her first love.

Chapter
2

Katie stood at the big glass doors and looked out at the ice-covered quad.

"I can't wait for it to warm up," Greg said. His arm tightened around her waist. "Rowing machines are okay for staying in shape, but they just don't cut it in terms of actual rowing. I'm *dying* to be out in a real boat, on the water, getting ready for the racing season."

Katie didn't answer. Her face was grim as she stared across the quad in the direction of the gymnasium.

"Hey, you promised," he said. "No negative thoughts. Why don't we go for a drive? The view from Rosemont Park must be terrific, now that the trees are bare."

Katie shook her head briefly. "I told some of the team I'd come by and watch them," she said. "Maybe I can help them choreograph their floor routines. At least I'd be doing *something* useful."

"Of course you would," Greg said quickly. "You're still Kennedy's best gymnast, even if you are on the injured list for a little while."

"For what's left of the season, you mean." She banged her looseleaf notebook against one of her crutches. "The rest of my senior year. The rest of my high school career. I would have done really well, Greg," she added in a smaller voice. She looked up at him sadly. "I was ready to win that championship again."

"Sure you were. Everybody knows that. It was just rotten luck, that's all."

"It was rotten *judgment*, and you know it. I never should have suggested going down that slope. I deserved to fall, but I don't think I deserved a broken leg." She gave a deep sigh and took a firmer grip on her crutches. "Come on. At the rate I move on these things, we're likely to miss practice altogether."

Greg slung her knapsack over his shoulder and reached to take her notebook as well.

"I'll carry it myself," she said. "I may be injured, but I'm not totally helpless."

He studied her face for a moment, then nodded and opened the door.

Katie was instantly sorry that she hadn't let Greg take the notebook. The walk had been plowed right after the snowstorm, but here and there, snow had drifted back onto it, melted in the sunlight, and frozen overnight into patches of ice smooth and slippery enough for a skating rink. When one of her crutches landed on such a patch, the rubber tip skittered right off, nearly making her fall.

She stopped and tried to breathe normally. All her life she had been doing cartwheels and flips, dancing along balance beams, and whirling on the parallel bars. Like any gymnast, she had taken some spills and collected some bruises, too, but she had always shrugged them off. They weren't important.

Now, just the thought of falling terrified her. Her gymnast's body, which she had always taken so much for granted, suddenly felt incredibly fragile. What if she broke her other leg? Or compounded the break she already had? She might be on crutches for months, and never do gymnastics again!

Greg misunderstood her reluctance. "Come on, everyone on the team is looking forward to seeing you," he said. "Everybody's pulling for you. And I know they'll be glad to have you help with the routines. They all know that if it hadn't been for you, nobody at Kennedy would even know we *had* a gymnastics team."

"I'm not — " She stopped herself. She couldn't tell Greg what she was really concerned about. She knew her leg would mend, even if it took longer than she wanted it to, and Katie knew the rest of the team liked and respected her. What really worried her was her fear that she had lost her nerve.

Once she got rid of her cast, a regimen of training, practice, and exercise would put her back in top condition. But condition only counted for about eighty percent. The other twenty percent, the part that separated a good gymnast from a champion, was confidence and attitude. Before her skiing accident, she had *known* that her mind and body would do exactly what she wanted them to. Now she wasn't so sure. Maybe she would fall. And even the tiniest of doubts might dull the edge of her performance — the edge she needed to be a winner.

She set her jaw and began to walk across the quad, carefully choosing each spot where she placed her crutches. Greg matched her cautious pace.

"I'm starting to get psyched for the tourney coming up," he said.

Katie looked blank.

"The debate tournament down at Charlottesville," he said. "I told you about it. It's going to be a very high-powered meet from what I hear. All the top debating teams in the region will be there."

"It's terrific that you were invited," Katie said. "This is the first time, isn't it?"

"Mmhmm. I hope we can hold our own." He grinned. "We're not what you'd call a seasoned team. It'd be great to win, of course, but I'll be ready to celebrate if we even manage to make the finals."

"Oh, you will. Of course you will!"

"If we get enough moral support. . . . So what do you say?"

"About what?"

"About coming down to watch us nail some of those hotshot debaters, of course!" She opened her mouth to protest, but he put a finger to her lips. "No, don't say anything. You can come down after school that Friday, catch some of the early rounds, and stay for the finals on Saturday."

"I'm not part of the team," she pointed out. "Where would I stay?"

"In a dorm, I guess. Look, Sasha Jenkins is at UVA, right? If she can't put you up, she'll find somebody who can. We can call her tonight."

"Well. . . ."

"Besides, it's not all boring arguments and counter-arguments, you know," he said, smiling. "There'll be a party Friday night after the debates, and on Saturday there's a big victory celebration. It really adds up to supporting your school, getting a taste of college life, giving the guy who loves you the encouragement he needs — "

"Since when do you need encouragement?" Katie demanded with a grin.

" — and two chances to party in one weekend . . . away from home." He raised his eyebrows comically. She had to laugh.

"And, of course, debates are very educational," he added. "You can learn a lot — about logic and constructing arguments. . . ."

She gave him a teasing glance. "And partying?"

"Very important," he said solemnly. "Social skills are essential to every profession, don't you think?"

"What *I* think," she replied, "is that you are the most lovable debater I know."

She turned to put her arms around his neck and give him a kiss. But the instant she let go of her crutches, she felt her one good foot slip on the icy walk. She let out a cry and grabbed for Greg's

17

shoulders. The one thing she must not do, no matter what, was put her weight on the cast. She twisted at the waist, as if she were about to land from a slightly mistimed back flip, but nothing worked the way it should. The extra weight of the plaster cast on her leg dragged her down, and the unfamiliar heaviness threw off her sense of balance. She felt herself toppling helplessly toward the concrete walk.

Then Greg's arms were encircling her waist, holding her safe. "Oops," he said cheerfully. "That was close."

Katie turned her head and rested her cheek against his chest. All the frustration and pain and anger she had tried so hard to ignore welled up in her. Tears burned her eyes, and she began to push Greg away.

"Idiot," she said through clenched teeth. "Idiot, idiot, *idiot!*"

"I'm not *that* bad," Greg cracked. Then he realized that it wasn't the time for jokes. Greg lifted his arm from Katie's waist to her shoulders and stroked her hair with his other hand. "It's all right, K.C.," he murmured in her ear. "It's all right."

"No, it isn't," she insisted, her voice muffled by his embrace. "It isn't all right at all. It's awful. I *hate* it!"

"Sure you do. But you can handle it. You're a fighter. Are you going to let a broken leg make you roll over and play dead? Not a chance!"

She leaned back and looked up at his face. She saw his concern for her and the confidence he had in her reflected in his features. For a moment she felt herself soften. But then her fear and sadness returned. What good was his concern? He didn't understand what she was going through!

"That's easy to say," she snapped. "How would you feel if you broke *your* leg tomorrow? And what if you knew you wouldn't be able to row for the rest of the year, and maybe forever? What if you'd been thinking about practically nothing else but crew, and racing, since you were eight years old? Could *you* handle it?"

Greg shook his head. "I don't know," he said. "I really don't. But I know one thing, Katie. If that happened to me, you'd want me to handle it, and you'd want to help me handle it, even if you didn't know how. And you'd keep at it, even if I resented your help sometimes."

"Greg Montgomery, you're impossible!" Her face was still streaked with tears, but the beginnings of a smile lurked in her eyes. "Why do you have to be so understanding? Can't you tell when I need to be mad at you?"

"I guess I'm not understanding enough for that," he said easily. "Besides, I don't want you mad at me. I'm going to need lots of positive energy from you next weekend at Charlottesville."

"Charlottesville," she sighed. "I don't know how *I* can go to Charlottesville. I can't even manage to get across the quad! If I didn't have you and Holly to help me, I couldn't get from one class to the next. And the doctor said I won't be ready for a walking cast for another two weeks. Two weeks — I can't *stand* it."

He tightened his arms again. "Come on," he said, "I know it's hard, but you're doing a great job. You're already getting around a lot better than you were a week ago. Once you get the walking cast, I bet you'll want to take up skateboarding."

She couldn't help smiling at the picture of herself whizzing down the sidewalk on a skateboard, cast and all.

"That's better," he continued. "And as for the debate tourney, I saw Karen Davis after lunch today. She and Brian Pierson are planning to drive down after school on Friday to cover it for WKND and *The Red and the Gold*. They'll be glad to give you a ride."

"You asked them already?"

"Sure. I want you to come. And not just for the parties, either." He hesitated for a moment, then his words tumbled out. "Competing won't be the same without you there to share it. And if I do well, I'll need you there so we can celebrate. What's a celebration without the girl I love?"

She felt a sudden flood of love for him. "Oh, Greg," she said. "Of course I'll come. And if the judges are too dumb to give you a prize, I'll crawl up on stage and hit them with my crutch."

"Sure," he said with a laugh, "you do that! And speaking of crutches. . . ."

He bent down and retrieved the fallen crutch while she balanced on her good leg and the other crutch. It wasn't that hard to do. Why was she worrying so much? On the balance beam she could go up on the ball of one foot and stand motionless for a minute at a time. Not with a cast on her leg, of course, but her strength and skill and muscle control ought to be good for *some-thing*.

"Hey," she said, giving Greg a poke, "let's get moving, Montgomery. I'm going to be late for practice."

He grinned and handed her the other crutch. "Last one to the gym is a rotten egg," he declared, and started hopping up the walk on one foot. On the fourth or fifth hop he lost his footing and tumbled head-first into a pile of snow.

For a moment, Katie was paralyzed with fear. Then she became angry as she saw him sit up and begin to brush off the snow. "Was that supposed to be funny?" she exclaimed. "You could hurt yourself fooling around like that!" But when Greg started laughing, she realized how silly she must have sounded. She gave him a sheepish smile.

He hovered near her, ready to help, all the way to the gym, and got her settled on the bottom row of bleachers, her crutches within easy reach.

"Are you all set?" he asked.

She nodded.

"Great. I'm going to put in some time in the library, but I'll come back for you at four-thirty, okay?"

She nodded again. He leaned over for a quick kiss, and then he was gone.

She moved her cast-encased leg to a slightly less uncomfortable position and started to watch the afternoon practice. She studied each of the girls on the team in turn, looking for awkward moves that needed work and good moves that needed emphasis. Half her mind was engaged that way — analyzing, comparing, working out new routines.

The other half was thinking over Greg's comment about competition. Of course it was better when you had someone there to share it with: teammates, coaches, friends. But at that moment, she felt she would give anything to be able to compete again, even if no one else realized it, or cared.

For a moment, tears pooled in her eyes. She brushed them away with determination. No matter how frustrating the next few weeks got, she was not going to give way to self-pity. It wouldn't do her any good, and it certainly wouldn't get her back in competition any sooner.

She focused once more on the activity in the gym. Her teammates needed her, now more than ever, and she was going to give them all the help she could. They deserved nothing less than her personal best.

Chapter
3

As the last notes of the new Huey Lewis song faded out, Brian Pierson said, "All right, Cardinals, that's it for Huey for the time being. Now let's pay a visit to the cutting edge of noise. Here's a band that's too new to be now. They call themselves Project Tomorrow, and the title of the number is 'Seven.' Or maybe I should say the number of the title is 'Seven.' Either way, give a listen to Project Tomorrow."

Holly sighed. She liked Brian, but she usually didn't think much of the new age music he played on his noontime show. The phrase he had used, "the cutting edge of noise," was usually pretty accurate. His favorite new bands tended to sound as if the drummer had tripped and knocked all the drums into the guitarist's amplifier. Project Tomorrow sounded like that, with the additional sound effects of a 747 taking off.

Jonathan Preston, across the table, met her eye

and smiled. "It makes you miss Peter Lacey, doesn't it?" Peter, who had graduated in June, had been WKND's star DJ for three years.

Holly nodded. "I'm just starting to realize how much! He really kept us in touch with what was happening in music."

Jonathan glanced toward the speaker in the ceiling of the lunchroom. "Maybe *this* is what's happening now."

Dee Patterson set her tray down, then put her camera down next to it. "Hey, what's happening?" she said.

"That's what we were trying to decide," Holly replied.

"I'm putting my money on the decline and fall of popular music," Jonathan said.

Dee made a face. "You call this popular? I know what I call it."

"Not at the table, please," Jonathan cracked. "Say, that was a great shot you took of Katie and Greg at the Valentine's Day Dance."

"Where was the picture?" asked Holly. "In the paper?"

"Uh-huh," Dee said. "It ran in last week's issue. I'm not surprised you missed it, though. It ended up pretty small."

The three of them stopped talking to say hello to their friend Matt. The table, reserved by tradition for the crowd of seniors who kept things going at Kennedy, was filling up fast.

Holly turned back to talk to Dee. "I'll look for it," she said.

"What?" said Matt, leaning to peer down at the floor under the table. "Did you lose something?"

"No, we were talking about Dee's picture from the dance," Holly explained with a laugh. "I missed it in the paper last week."

"By the way," Jonathan said, "what are you going to do with the rest of the pictures you took? It seemed like every time I turned around, I saw your flash going off."

Dee smiled. "News photographers figure they're doing well if they get one really good shot per roll."

"But you must have taken more than one roll."

"True. Maybe I'll offer the best of my candids to the yearbook. Some of them *are* pretty candid."

Jonathan grinned. "You mean you got some photos of people who really *liked* their computer Valentines?" Jonathan was referring to the four "fixed" dates Roxanne arranged for herself with Eric, Matt, Greg, and himself.

Dee grinned back. "I caught some real romantic matchmaking in action. I'm not naming any names, of course, but the faces speak for themselves."

Holly stiffened. What if one of Dee's pictures showed her with Zachary? Not close up, because she would have noticed her taking it, but maybe in the background? Or what if Dee had her telephoto lens that night? Everyone who looked at the yearbook would see the picture, everyone who knew Holly would know it was her, and *somebody* would certainly show it to Bart. He would flip out. He might never speak to her again. And whatever he did in response, Diana would follow his lead. She had made that clear already.

Suddenly Diana sat down at the other end of

the table, across from Pamela. She didn't look at Holly or even seem to realize that she was there, but Holly knew better. She could recognize a cold shoulder when she met one. She wasn't the only one to notice, either. Emily, who wrote the "Candy Hearts" advice column in *The Red and the Gold*, looked at Diana, then at Holly, and seemed about to say something, then changed her mind. And when Jeremy, Diana's English boyfriend, arrived at the table, he took in the situation at once and gave Holly a sympathetic glance as he sat down next to Diana.

"Maybe we should put up a display of pictures from the dance," Jonathan continued, "showing some computer match-ups, and mismatches, too!"

Holly wished she could just fade away and disappear. She could feel Diana's eyes glaring at her from across the table.

Dee smiled. "Sure. We could even use it to raise money for charity. A ten-dollar contribution guarantees that your photo won't be in the show."

"No, I'm serious," Jonathan insisted. "Everybody's under so much pressure to pair off these days. Maybe it keeps us from getting to know each other better. You know how it is. All a guy has to do is talk to some girl for more than ten minutes, and everyone figures they're going together. Wouldn't it be great if it were all right to be friends with somebody of the opposite sex, even if there isn't any romantic interest — even if both people are dating other people?" he said sarcastically.

"Watch out, everybody," Matt said. "Jonathan's getting another one of his ideas."

Over the laughter, Jonathan said, "You just may be right! Look, why aren't there any of the Stevenson kids at the table?"

There was an awkward silence.

"Is it because we deliberately exclude them? Of course not! Nobody wants to do that. The problem is that we don't know most of them, and they don't know us. Why?"

Dee said, "We've been in school together for years, and they're new around here."

"Right," said Jonathan. "And that's why it's up to us to fix the situation. We have to go out of our way to get to know more of them, whether they're guys or girls. Whether you're seeing someone or not. We have to make them our friends; they're Kennedy kids now."

Holly kept her eyes fixed on her plate. She was afraid that if she raised her head, she would find Diana still staring at her accusingly. What Jonathan was talking about was just too coincidental to what had happened between her and Zachary. Diana might even think that Holly had put him up to it.

"So what's the solution?" Jeremy asked in a skeptical voice. "Another computer dating plan?"

The laughter around the table was tinged with embarrassment. None of them liked to recall the way Roxanne Easton had manipulated all of them at the Valentine's Day Dance. Jonathan and Matt, who had both been victims of her scheme, reddened.

"I just want to make sure we're all aware of the problem," Jonathan replied. "I don't know what the answer is. Not yet, anyway. But I'm working on it."

Holly scuffled slowly across the snowy campus toward the gym. She had waited until most people had left for the day, because she wanted to make sure that no one she knew saw her talking to Zachary. She had avoided him since finding out that Diana knew about their kiss at the Valentine's Day Dance, but she couldn't go on avoiding him forever. It wasn't fair to keep him in the dark. She had to find him, face him, and tell him it was all over between them — what little there was.

It was a shame that Zack had developed such a huge crush on her, Holly thought. He was a nice, sweet, interesting guy — someone she would have liked to have as a friend. But that was impossible now. She was afraid that, with the way he felt about her, any attempt she made to be friendly would seem as if she were encouraging him. And she couldn't take the risk of keeping up a relationship that Diana, and others, might misinterpret.

It was so complicated having her boyfriend's sister as her best friend. She wanted more than anything to talk to Diana, to tell her what had been going on, and get her reactions and advice. She needed to hear another point of view from someone who wasn't as deeply involved as she was. But of course Diana *was* involved. Because what Holly had done would hurt Bart, she had hurt his sister as well. Holly knew that, and she was sorry for it. But at that moment, she was sorrier that she didn't have a different best friend to give her the support she needed.

When she got to the gym, Zack didn't seem to be anywhere in sight. That surprised her. She had thought that he worked out every day after school, but apparently he took a day off now and then. She couldn't ask anyone if they'd seen him, though, because she didn't want to call attention to the fact that she was looking for him. She wandered listlessly down the corridor, past display cases filled with trophies and plaques. She wasn't due at her job at the medical clinic until five, and she decided to drop by the sub shop for half an hour or so.

She paused on the steps of the gym and took a deep breath. Most of the snow had melted, and the breeze carried a faint smell of wet earth, hinting that spring was not so very far away. Her heart leaped up into her throat. What was more wonderful than spring when you were in love, or more desolate than spring when you were apart from the one you loved? And which did the approaching spring hold for her?

She started off toward the sub shop. As she passed the football field, she saw three or four people working out. She recognized the number on one of the red and gold jerseys — it was Zachary's. She started toward him, but as she got closer her footsteps slowed. All day she had been rehearsing in her head the words she meant to say, but now they had all escaped her. She knew why. However carefully she said what she had to say, she was going to hurt Zack a lot, and he had done nothing at all to deserve being hurt. But she had to do it.

* * *

29

Zachary finished a series of wind sprints and straightened up, hands on hips, breathing in huge gulps. In spite of the cold air, sweat was pouring down his face. He took the towel from around his neck and mopped his forehead and cheeks. In the few weeks since the football season and the daily team workouts had ended, he had felt himself starting to fall off from peak condition. He had begun working out on his own — it was important to him to be in good shape, and he knew being in shape would make it easier for him to get back into playing condition when team workouts started again.

He tucked the towel back into his sweat shirt and pulled his shoulders back. It was time to practice some broken field running: five yards, then break right; another five yards and break left. He had gotten about halfway down the field when he stopped and straightened up. Someone was coming from the direction of the gym, and he was ninety percent sure that someone was Holly Daniels. He swallowed. She could only be coming to see *him*.

Even through his sudden excitement, he was surprised that she was seeking him out. He didn't understand why she seemed to want to keep their friendship such a secret. She didn't even like him saying hello when they passed each other in the hall. Was it because he was only a junior? He knew that a lot of girls felt funny about getting involved with a guy who was younger than they were, even if it was only by a couple of months. Maybe that was what was bothering Holly.

Or maybe Roxanne was right. She was telling

people that the crowd that ran things at Kennedy had decided to freeze out the kids who had transferred from Stevenson. According to her, their only hope of having a say in what happened at school was to unite behind her and insist on having some voice about the way things were run. Zack wasn't too interested in who ran the school paper or the radio station or the student government. But what if the Kennedy crowd wanted to freeze out the Stevenson kids athletically and socially, too? Holly was part of that crowd. She might not want her friends to know she liked someone from Stevenson, for fear of what they would say.

He looked down and groaned. His sweat shirt was all sweaty, and he was carrying about half the mud on the football field on his cleats and sweat pants. Holly was coming to see him, and he looked as if he had just lost a mud-wrestling match.

But that didn't really matter. The important thing was that Holly had come looking for him. Practice forgotten, he raced across the field to meet her. She stopped by the stands and waited for him.

"Hi," he said when he was still a dozen feet away.

"Hi," Holly said in a small voice.

He came up to her and reached out to give her a hug, but she took a quick step backward. He dropped his arms and frowned. "Is anything wrong?" he asked, then added, "I guess I am pretty dirty."

"It's not that." Holly looked over her shoulder

as if afraid that someone might see her. When she turned back, she refused to meet his eyes.

Zack's heart sank. "Something *is* wrong, isn't it?" he said.

"Uh-huh. It's. . . ." Her voice got so quiet that he had to strain to hear her. "Look, Zachary," she continued, "I can't see you anymore."

"You can't — " He couldn't make himself finish the sentence.

"I'm sorry," Holly said.

"I don't understand. What did I do?"

She shook her head. "Nothing. It's all my problem." Her eyes glistened in the pale winter sunlight. "I should have told you right at the start. I've been going with somebody else for a long time, over a year. His name's Bart Einerson and he's off at college now, but he'll be back soon. I don't know how I let this happen, but I know it's got to stop right now, before it goes any further and hurts a lot of people."

"But haven't you hurt me already?" he snapped angrily. He was so confused and upset he didn't realize how sharp his words sounded until he saw Holly flinch.

"You have a right to be mad," she said softly. "I know it must have seemed as if I *wanted* to get involved with you. I was feeling lonely, and I thought you were very sweet and very attractive." She smiled briefly. "You are, too," she added. "But I didn't think it through. It was wrong to encourage you when I knew it couldn't go anywhere."

Tears were trickling down her cheeks. Despite his pain and anger, he saw that she was upset, too.

He thought about how much he liked Holly. They had become so close in their few short times together. Every night since the Valentine's Day Dance he had gone to sleep remembering their kiss. Could he let something so important be taken away from him just like that?

"Don't cry, Holly, it's all right." He reached out a hand to pat her shoulder but pulled it back. She might misunderstand the gesture. "Look, I understand about you going with this other guy. I didn't know, that's all. We can still be friends, can't we?"

She shook her head again, more violently this time. "Oh, Zack," she said. "I don't think it would work out." Her lower lip began to tremble. She swallowed a couple of times before continuing. "I made a big mistake. It isn't fair that you're the one who has to pay for it, but I can't help it. If we try to be friends, it'll just make it harder for both of us."

"But I won't — " he began.

For the first time she looked up to meet his eyes. The pain he saw in her face made him want to hold and comfort her, but he knew that wasn't what she wanted.

"I — " She bit her lips for a long moment, then said, "I'm sorry, Zack." She whirled around and walked away very quickly. He stood and watched, but she never turned back to look at him.

"McGraw, you dope," he muttered. He should have seen it coming, he told himself. How could he have expected a girl like Holly — a senior; bright, pretty, part of the important crowd at Kennedy — to be interested in him?

He recognized Bart Einerson's name. He had probably played against him in a Kennedy–Stevenson game. He knew that Bart had been a star athlete while he was at Kennedy. But he would have been well-known anyway. His father was a congressman, which made him an instant celebrity, and he was the kind of smart, funny, smooth guy who always had plenty of girls hanging around him.

And what am *I*? Zack thought bitterly. A junior with so-so grades. My only distinction is that I play football well. A dumb jock, in other words. No wonder Holly dumped me so fast. Bart had good grades, too. Zack McGraw was not the kind of guy she needed to be seen with if she wanted to stay in good with her crowd. She had made a mistake? Well, so had he. He had thought that he had a chance to build something good with Holly. In reality, he had never had any chance at all.

Zack walked back toward the gym. It was about time for a good workout with a punching bag.

Chapter
4

Karen Davis tapped the ruler against her teeth and frowned down at her desk. She was in the middle of laying out the front page of the following week's issue of *The Red and the Gold*, and she had just run into a problem. Adam Tanner's interview with Ms. Murdock, the guidance counselor, was still about a hundred words too long for the space she had reserved for it. She had three choices. She could cut the article still more, continue it on an inside page, or rearrange her layout. But she had already edited out several paragraphs from the article, she disliked little one-inch continuations, and she had put a lot of work into creating a layout with a nice feeling of symmetry and didn't want to spoil it.

She sighed, picked up her blue pencil, and began to read through the article again, looking for sections to cut.

"Karen?" Dee called from the other side of the

room. "I think we've got a small problem." Pamela and Emily looked up from their work momentarily, but then relaxed when they realized it wasn't serious.

"That's the only kind of problem I like," Karen replied. "What is it?"

"The piece on the gymnastics meet. I checked the files for a photo, but all the good ones are of Katie Crawford."

"Um. And K.C. won't be in the meet. I see your point."

"I can trot over to the gym this afternoon and take some shots of the others," said Dee. "But it'll be pushing it to have one ready in time for this issue."

Karen flipped through a stack of papers and found the rough layout for the sports page. After studying it for a few moments, she said, "Okay, we'll scratch the gymnastics photo for now and try to run one next week from the meet. Dee, are you planning to cover it?"

"Yes," Dee responded.

"And did you get any good action shots at the swim meet?"

"Yeah, one or two." Dee found the photos and brought them over to Karen's desk.

One of Eric, with his face half out of water with one arm arching over, looked spectacular. They decided to run it, along with a picture of a racing start, and another of three contestants clinging to the edge of the pool, gasping for breath after finishing a race.

"I'll crop them and get them back to you after lunch," Dee said.

"Great."

The office door banged open. Karen looked up. Her boyfriend, Brian Pierson, was standing there with a broad smile on his face. "Guess what?" he demanded. "I just phoned home to check on the mail. I got into Brown!"

Karen jumped up from her desk. "Really? Brian, that's fantastic! Congratulations!" She ran over and gave him an enthusiastic kiss. His answering hug was so tight that she thought her ribs would crack.

"You don't have to sound so surprised," he teased. "After all, they let you in, didn't they?"

Karen blushed. She had been very proud of gaining early acceptance at Brown, her first-choice college, but she had been worried that Brian might not get in, too. She wanted to be at college with him, but she had her heart set on going to Brown, and would have been really upset if they couldn't be at college together. All of a sudden, that very big problem was no problem at all.

"Yippee!" she exclaimed, and gave him another kiss. He swung her off her feet, then set her down long enough to accept congratulations from Dee, Pamela, and Emily.

"That's terrific," Pamela said. "Isn't Brown one of the toughest schools to get into in the whole country?"

Brian struck a pose with his thumbs tucked into imaginary suspenders. "Hey," he said, "I'm *special*!" Then he ducked the pink eraser that Karen sent flying toward him. "You're special, too, Karen," he said laughing, reaching over to give her another hug.

"Hey," Pamela said. "It's lunchtime, Brian. Aren't you supposed to be on the air now? Who's minding the radio station?"

"No sweat," Brian replied with a wave of his hand. "You know Josh Ferguson? A junior? He came up with this great idea for a show with a different theme each week, so I'm giving him a chance to get behind the mike."

"What's the theme of the first show?" Pamela asked.

"Every song is going to have something to do with TV. He's got the Monkees, the *Dragnet* theme, even Partridge Family songs — "

"And the *Batman* theme, I hope," Emily added, giggling. "It sounds as if he'll work out."

"I hope so. The station needs somebody new." He put on a gangster movie scowl and snarled, "I'm busting outta dis joint pretty soon."

While they were laughing, he added, "Not that anybody could really replace me. Who else would take the trouble to try to raise the level of musical taste in this school?"

"Oh, is *that* what you're trying to do?" Pamela asked, teasing him. "I knew there had to be a reason why you played that kind of noise — er, *music*."

Brian growled and pretended to swipe at her, but she retreated to the layouts on her desk. Emily and Dee went back to their work, too, leaving Karen alone with Brian for the first time since she heard his news.

"Kidding aside," she said, "I'm really happy.

It couldn't have worked out better for us, could it?"

"Nope." He hesitated, then said softly, "I couldn't help worrying, especially after you got accepted. I don't want to be away from you, Karen."

She put her arms around his neck. "I feel the same way," she whispered, gazing deeply into his eyes. He lowered his lips onto hers, and she closed her eyes to savor every moment of their kiss.

Suddenly the door banged open again. "Is this the newspaper office?" a voice demanded.

Karen and Brian sprang apart. The guy in the doorway was no one Karen knew. His disheveled brown hair, scuffed cowboy boots, and piercing gaze would have marked him in her memory.

"That's right," she said. "Can I help you? Do you need something?"

"No, you do. You need some new blood around here. I'm Daniel Tackett," he said. "The former editor of the *Stevenson Sentinel*. Not that I expect anyone around here to care about that. We've already heard all about how the hotshots at Kennedy are planning to keep everything just the way it was before we poor refugees showed up."

"That's not fair," Karen began. "This whole situation is new for us, too. We're trying — "

Daniel interrupted her. "Do you know where I can find the editor of this insipid rag? Maybe there's a chance he'll know some real journalistic ideas when he hears them."

Karen worked very hard to keep her voice level, but her anger rang in every word. "First off, buddy, if you'd bothered to look at the masthead, you'd know that 'he' is a 'she.' Karen Davis, editor in chief. And you're talking to her . . . if that's what you call what you've been doing. All I've heard so far is a lot of hot air."

He faltered for a moment, but then recovered. "Sorry, I didn't get as far as the masthead," he said. "I fell asleep halfway through the front page. The motto around here is obviously, 'Dare to be boring!'"

Karen planted her hands on her hips and glared at him through narrowed eyes. "We run a responsible, professional newspaper here," she said. "We won an award last year, and we're not in business to keep you amused. I don't know what kind of stuff you ran in your paper, but around here we print *news*. What did you expect, UFO stories? Features on the latest horror flicks? 'Herd of unicorns found grazing in Kennedy soccer field'?"

"News?" Daniel gave a sarcastic laugh. "Prove it! What are you running in next week's paper?"

"It's none of your business," Karen said, "but here." She led him over to her desk and pointed to the layout she had just been working on. "Our lead article is about the debate team. They've come from nowhere to become one of the top teams in the whole region, and next week they're participating in an important invitational meet down in Charlottesville."

Daniel conspicuously stifled a yawn, then said, "What's your headline? 'Debate Team to Attend Big Meet'?"

Karen's face grew warm. His sarcastic suggestion was uncomfortably close to the headline she had been planning to use. "We're also running a humor piece about the foul-up with the computer Valentines," she said.

He didn't speak, but the look of disdain on his face said a lot.

"There's a feature on the Maple Sugarin' Festival at the Nature Center. We need to get our students behind it to make it a success, and it's going to be very interesting and informational, besides."

"Fascinating," he said.

Karen was beginning to feel a little desperate. She had just exhausted the front page. "On the sports page we have stories on the gymnastics team's first meet of the season, on the swim team, on this week's basketball games, and an announcement of baseball tryouts."

"Penetrating, hard-hitting journalism," he said. "And your lead editorial?"

"We're calling for a better system of informing students when the school has to be closed because of snow. People who called in to find out if school was open couldn't get through. So about a hundred kids actually showed up, then had to go home again."

"You really believe in going out on a limb for the things that matter," Daniel observed. "How many snow days did Kennedy have this winter?"

"Well . . . just two so far, but that's not the point. Kids shouldn't have to — "

"Get out of bed if school's closed that day," he said, finishing her sentence for her. "Okay, okay," he added when Karen began to protest. "I've made my point. The whole paper's nothing but fluff.

Debate teams, swim teams, gymnastics teams, tiddlywinks teams. Where's the stories that make people wake up and pay attention? What about making your readers *think*?"

"We don't — "

He raised his voice. "When was the last time you got the administration mad? Have they ever threatened to close you down?"

"Well — "

"Of course not! You know why? Because you never do anything to upset them. Your paper is just another part of the establishment. You help keep the student body passive and ignorant instead of educating and rousing them."

"You make it sound as if the only job of a paper is to get people angry about something — about anything," Karen said. "But we run stories that may show some people a part of Kennedy they might not have seen. We entertain them sometimes, we also try to inform them. You made fun of an article about baseball tryouts. But how are people going to find out about the tryouts if we don't tell them?"

Daniel shrugged, apparently unconcerned. "That could be a two-line announcement," he said. "Or they could put up a poster on the bulletin board." He looked at Brian for the first time. "Are you the sports editor?"

"I'm not on the paper," Brian replied. "I work at WKND."

"The radio station?" Daniel laughed derisively. "Lightweight! Take that lunchtime show, 'Soundings.' The music's okay, and the guy who does it finds some interesting stuff to play. But where's the hard news? Where's the open mike? What about group discussions of things that really matter to kids today? Nowhere! The station is just one more part of the nice cozy system around here, and nobody has the guts to shake it up and make it live up to its potential."

Brian had listened calmly to Daniel's remarks about *The Red and the Gold,* but the criticism of his show and his radio station stung him. "You've got a big mouth, Tackett," he said, clenching his fists. "You better take it somewhere else unless you want a fat lip to match it."

Daniel turned to face him, chin up and shoulders square. "Is that a threat?" he asked quietly.

"I'm not threatening you," Brian replied loudly. "I'm just telling you to get out of here before I throw you out."

"Brian — " Karen said.

"No, I mean it! This guy has no idea what you go through to put out a paper — or what I do to air a radio show — and he wants to teach us our business! If this guy knows so much, why doesn't he go put out his own newspaper?"

"I did, until they closed my school," Daniel said.

That silenced Brian for a moment. Karen said, "Listen, Daniel, if you — "

Brian broke in. "If you don't get out of this office right now, I'm going to drag you out!"

"Don't worry, sport, I'm leaving. I'm glad I came by. Now I know that it's just like everybody said. You Kennedy guys really are doing what you can to block us out. Go ahead, try it. But I'm telling you right now, it won't work."

As he turned to go, he reached into his backpack and tossed something on Karen's desk. "Here," he said. "Take a look at a *real* newspaper."

The door slammed.

"Whew!" said Karen, settling back against the edge of her desk.

"What a jerk!" Brian huffed.

"Daniel Tackett, last of the red-hot agitators," Emily said dryly.

Karen, meanwhile, had picked up the Stevenson paper and was scanning the front page.

"You know something?" she said a few moments later. "He put out a darn good paper. Here's an exposé on liquor stores that sell to minors. It names them, too."

"A student guide to buying booze?" Brian cracked.

"No, really," Karen insisted. "It names one store that sold alcohol to a Stevenson kid who then got drunk, drove into the median on the interstate, and nearly killed himself and a couple of other people, too. It's a good, solid, hard-hitting story. And here's an interview with someone who used to go to Stevenson, telling about his experience working on a project building schools in Central America. And a debate about whether teachers should have the right to strike."

"Let *me* look at that rag," Brian grumbled. He read in silence for a couple of minutes, then looked up. His face was troubled. "You're right," he said. "It's a good paper. A little heavy-handed and preachy, but good. And he's right, too. *The Red and the Gold* has gotten flabby."

44

"Fluffy was the word," Karen said in a grim voice. "But yeah, he was right. And we ordered him to get out of the office."

"That was my fault. He *is* a loud-mouth, but I blew my cool. We were in such a good mood until he came in and dragged us down."

Karen moved over to put her head on Brian's shoulder. "Never mind," she said softly. "Your news is still just as super as it was before."

Brian gave her a long, intense kiss. Afterward, as she rested her cheek against his chest, she said, "I know what I have to do."

"Hmm?"

"I have to find Daniel Tackett and talk him into doing something for the paper. He's a real pain, but he's also a real journalist. We can use him."

"Maybe so," Brian said. "But just watch out that he doesn't end up using *us*."

Chapter
5

Frankie Baker fidgeted with a strand of pale blonde hair, twisting it nervously around her finger. "I don't really have time this afternoon, Rox," she said. "Anyway, I'm not hungry."

Roxanne Easton sighed and rolled her eyes. "Hungry isn't the point," she replied. "The sub shop is where all the important people from Kennedy hang out after school. It's the place to be, hungry or not. That's why I'm dropping by, and that's why you're coming along."

"But — "

"Look, Frankie, I'm trying to do you a favor. You don't want to spend the rest of your life standing on the outside looking in, do you?"

For one moment Frankie was tempted to say yes. Sometimes it seemed easier to stay on the outside rather than overcome her shyness and insecurity. But she knew that wasn't really where she wanted to be. "No, of course not," she murmured, looking down.

"Okay, then. I'm doing my best to get you into the swing of things, but I need cooperation from you. Come on, you can give me a lift home afterward."

As she drove to the sub shop, Frankie found herself wishing once again that she hadn't been forced to transfer to Kennedy High School. She knew the other kids at Stevenson — she'd been in the same classes with some of them since elementary school. Frankie knew she was shy, but it had never seemed too much of a problem until she had had to start the painful, awkward process of getting to know a whole new bunch of Kennedy kids. Roxanne was different. She wasn't afraid to talk to anyone or go anywhere. Without Roxanne, Frankie would never have had the courage to go to a student hangout where she wasn't going to know a soul. In fact, if Roxanne hadn't been around to encourage her, there were a lot of things Frankie wouldn't have done.

Roxanne was unusually silent. Was it possible she was nervous, too? Didn't Roxanne already know a lot of the "in" kids? Frankie was trying to work out a diplomatic way to ask, when her friend suddenly said, "I can't believe how selfish they are!"

"Selfish?" Frankie repeated. "Who?"

"All of them. The whole Kennedy crowd. What makes them think they're so special? Just because they've been around that school long enough to run everything!" She fell silent again, then burst

47

out, "You know what the problem really is? They're afraid of us! They don't want new faces, new ideas, people who'll rock the boat. They want to keep everything just the way it was before we showed up. That's why they're trying to pretend we don't exist."

Frankie frowned. Rox had said this sort of thing before, and she still didn't know how to respond to it. To her, the kids at Kennedy seemed pretty much like the kids at Stevenson: A few of them ignored her, some went out of their way to be nice, and most of them were somewhere in between.

"What really gets to me," Roxanne continued, "is that I came so close. I'd worked it out so carefully. If Katie Crawford hadn't interfered, you'd see the Kennedy kids treating us with a lot more respect."

"Interfered in what?" asked Frankie, puzzled.

"The whole business at the dance. *You* know."

Frankie reddened. She certainly did know. The program for computer-matching people at the Valentine's Day Dance had been her idea, and running it had been her responsibility, although Roxanne took all the glory for it. Frankie told Jonathan and the others that her program would match everyone who filled out the questionnaire with a secret Valentine. The questionnaires, and their revealing personal information, would be kept strictly confidential.

On the whole, it had worked just the way she said it would. Most of the kids at the dance had a great time. They loved going to a mysterious rendezvous and murmuring the secret code words that identified them to their computer-chosen dates. Some of the pairings were romantic, and some were hilarious, but almost all of them were fun.

Almost all. Unknown to everyone else, Roxanne had talked Frankie into letting her see the questionnaires filled out by Matt Jacobs, Jonathan Preston, and a couple of other guys. She read what each of them had said they wanted in a girl, then used what she learned to turn herself into each guy's ideal date. That was bad enough, but later, when Frankie was printing out the computer matchings, Roxanne had made her rig the program. The result was that Rox became the secret Valentine of four different guys. She came very close to pulling it off, too, until the guys somehow found out what was going on. Instead of being the social success of the night, she ended up getting the cold shoulder from everyone. And Frankie, naturally, felt terribly embarrassed and responsible for the whole mess.

"But Rox," Frankie protested. "Your plan didn't work, that's all. Katie Crawford didn't have anything to do with it."

"That's what you think. After that skiing accident, she went around telling everyone that the accident had been my fault. Can you imagine? *She* picked the hardest trail on the slope and so it wasn't any surprise that I fell down. And just because her ex-boyfriend and a few other guys were sweet enough to try and help me, does that mean I'm to blame if Eric fell in front of her and tripped her up? But that's what she's telling people. See what I mean? We can't expect fair treatment from them. They're in for a surprise, though. They won't have Roxanne Easton to kick around anymore. I'm going to beat them at their own game."

Frankie gripped the steering wheel tighter. She had watched Roxanne carry out her plots before, and she knew someone usually got hurt. "How are you going to do that?" she asked, glancing over at her friend. Rox was wearing a little smile that promised trouble for someone.

"I've got my eye on Greg Montgomery," she announced.

"Katie's boyfriend? But — "

"Star debater," Roxanne continued dreamily, "captain of the varsity crew, tall and handsome, lives in a huge house over on Cliffside Avenue, drives a yummy white Mercedes. . . . Face it, he's the grand prize in the junior class sweepstakes. He deserves something better than helping Katie the Cripple get from one class to the next."

"That's mean, Rox! You shouldn't talk like that."

"Oh, come off it, Frankie," Roxanne said coldly. "Why not? I bet they call us names all the time."

Frankie was flustered by Roxanne's attitude. "Yeah, but. . . . Well, if I broke my leg, I'd want my boyfriend to stand by me and help me. Wouldn't you?"

"Not if our relationship was over," said Roxanne. "It wouldn't be right to try to hold him then. I'd want to set him free to find someone who could be more important to him."

"But they look like they're really in love!"

Roxanne shook her head: "I can't say any more, Frankie. I don't want to betray any confidences. There's a lot I could tell you, but it wouldn't be right. Oh, look," she added in a more animated voice, "there's the sub shop! Pull in over there."

Frankie stopped just inside the door and looked around. The sub shop was so cluttered with memorabilia, Frankie couldn't remember what she'd seen the first time she was there with Rox. From across the room, a larger-than-life-size stuffed bear looked ready to spring — or fall apart, whichever came first. A motorcycle was mounted high on the back wall, and from the ceiling dangled rows of Kennedy High School football pennants. Some of them were very faded, evidence of the long connection between Kennedy and the sub shop.

At the moment, they were just about the only evidence of that connection. The place was nearly empty. Half a dozen kids were sitting around one of the picnic tables at the rear, but when she looked, she realized they were Stevenson kids, too.

If the Kennedy crowd's absence disappointed Roxanne, she didn't let it show. "I'm starved," she announced, heading for the counter. "I hope the fries are good."

Frankie had known Roxanne since fourth grade, and by now she was used to Rox's impulsive way of changing her plans. She followed her over to the counter and ordered a soda she didn't want, then joined Roxanne in a booth. "How are the fries?" Frankie asked after a minute or two.

"Soggy," Roxanne replied, making a face. She turned her head to survey the place. "Do you think they really hang out here? I can't imagine why. I'd give it about an eight on the yuckola scale myself."

"Maybe the food isn't the main attraction," Frankie observed. "It's probably just a place to hang out." Rox gave her a sharp look. Frankie suddenly recalled that Rox had said something similar earlier, about the important kids hanging out here. She hoped Roxanne didn't think she was making fun of her. She didn't want Rox angry at her. Without her, Frankie might never get to know anyone! To hide her confusion, she bent over her glass of soda and took a sip.

What was she doing at the sub shop anyway? Waiting for her back at home was a new graphics program that was supposed to have some amazing capabilities. She had just gotten it the night before and wanted to get home so she could try it out.

Roxanne was not going to like having to leave before she wanted to. She never liked doing anything she didn't want to. "Gee, I'm sorry," Frankie began carefully. "I don't want to rush you, but I'm going to have to go home real soon. I just remembered that — "

She stopped in midsentence and caught her breath. Her stomach felt as if she had stepped onto an express elevator going down. Zachary McGraw had just walked in the door, and he was looking around with a forlorn expression on his face.

Roxanne noticed Frankie's reaction and turned to see what had caused it. She turned back to Frankie and demanded, "Really, Frankie. You don't still have that silly crush on Zachary, do you?"

Frankie looked down at the table, blushing furiously. "I never said I had a crush on him," she said. "He's a nice guy, that's all."

"Sure, sure," Rox said. She seemed about to say more, but instead, she turned on a smile as Zack came over to their table.

Frankie's cheeks were burning. She looked up at him for an instant, then dropped her eyes in terror. She knew she was acting like the most childish, awkward, self-conscious person on earth, but she couldn't help it. She wished a trap door would open under her chair and give her a way to escape.

"Hello, Zachary," Roxanne said sweetly. "I've really missed seeing you lately. Where have you been hiding?"

"I'm in training," he mumbled. "Trying to stay in shape for the fall."

"Fantastic," Roxanne declared. "I wish more people had that kind of dedication. I think it's the real secret to being a top-flight athlete. Lots of people have some ability, but how many put the kind of effort into it that you do?"

While Rox was speaking, Zack was looking around the room. When she finished, he said, "This *is* the place where the Kennedy crowd hangs out, isn't it?"

Rox frowned. Zack seemed not to have heard a word she said. "That's what they say," she replied. "They're not hanging out here now, though. Are you looking for anybody special?"

"Hmm?" he said, not looking at her.

"Who were you hoping to meet here? Anybody we know?"

He shook his head but still didn't meet Roxanne's eyes. "Nobody special," he said. "I was just curious."

Frankie summoned up enough courage to say, "Would you like to sit down?"

"Sure," Rox added. "Pull over a chair."

He shifted uncertainly from one foot to the other. "Well, actually, I sort of wanted to ask Franko about something. I guess it can wait, though."

Frankie stared at the straw wrapper lying on the table. She knew Rox's eyes were on her, studying her shrewdly. Her face felt hot.

"Hey, don't mind me," Rox said. Her voice was still sweet, but something told Frankie that she was boiling mad. "I see somebody over there I need to talk to."

She stood up and walked away. The moment she was gone, Zack slipped into the booth in her place and gave Frankie a friendly smile. "Was I rude?" he asked. "I know she's your friend, but Rox and I don't get along too well."

"That's okay," Frankie said, too softly to be heard. She cleared her throat and repeated, "That's okay."

"Oh, good." He fell silent and began to draw on the tabletop with one of Rox's leftover French fries. Then he realized what he was doing and dropped it hurriedly. "I never got to thank you," he said. "About the dance, I mean."

"That's okay," she said once more, then blushed

even harder. She was starting to sound like a stuck record. "I'm glad it worked out."

No one — not even Roxanne — knew that Frankie had rigged the computer Valentines to match Zachary with Holly Daniels. She still wasn't sure if she had done the right thing. But he had confided in her, told her how much he liked the Kennedy girl, and asked for her help. How could she have refused him?

"It *didn't* work out," he said in a morose voice. "I thought it had, but after the dance Holly kept avoiding me. I didn't push it — I thought maybe she was feeling shy about letting her friends see her with me. But that wasn't it."

"No? What was it?"

"She's going with somebody else, and has been for a long time."

"Oh, Zack!" She impulsively reached across the table and put her hand on top of his. "How awful for you! But who is he? Why didn't you know?" She looked down at her hand, not quite understanding why it was touching Zack's. Suddenly realizing what she'd done, she yanked it away. Frankie was amazed at how comfortable she was around Zack, once they were just talking one-on-one.

Zack seemed not to have noticed her hand on his. "Bart's his name," he went on. "Bart Einerson. He's Holly's best friend's brother. He's away at college now, but he's coming back pretty soon."

"Oh. So that's why she — "

"Uh-huh." He picked up another cold French fry and nibbled at it moodily. "It's not fair," Zack said suddenly. "I know she can't start anything with me when she's got a regular boyfriend. I accept that. But why won't she let us be friends? I like her a whole lot, and I think she likes me, too, but she says she won't even talk to me again. Can you figure that out, Franko?"

She had an idea, but it wasn't one she was ready to tell him about. What if Holly liked Zack too much to trust herself to be around him? If she were Holly, Frankie could imagine herself feeling like that.

"Maybe I'm just too dumb for her," Zachary continued. "Her boyfriend is a good student. He even starred in a play when he was here! He must have a whole bunch of interesting things to talk about with her. Me, I can't seem to find *anything* to say to her. I try, but nothing comes to me. You want to know how I met her? I was in the library, trying to put a reel in the microfilm reader. I couldn't figure it out at all until she came over and showed me."

"Had you ever used one of the machines before?" Frankie asked.

"I'd never even seen one before. But so what? A sixth-grader should've been able to figure it out. Not me. No wonder she thinks I'm stupid. She's right."

Frankie wished she had Holly Daniels there so she could tell her what she thought of her. No one had the right to make a sweet guy like Zack feel so bad about himself! And as for him, she wished she could give him a good shaking. How could he let anyone make him feel so worthless?

But he had come to her as a friend for friendly

advice. She didn't dare tell him what she'd been thinking — it might reveal too much about how she felt about him.

"*I* think you're interesting," she said. "And you're certainly not dumb. You don't get to be all-city quarterback by being dumb."

"That's football. I'm talking about other things."

"Look, before an important game, do you try to figure out the other team — what they're like, how best to score against them?

"Well, why not do the same thing with Holly Daniels? You want to be interesting to her? Find out what *she's* interested in, and learn something about it. You don't have to know much, just enough to get her talking about whatever it is."

Zachary thought for a minute, then said, "Sure, I get it. That's a terrific idea. Thanks, Franko, you're a real pal!"

That's what I'm afraid of, Frankie thought. But she would rather be Zack's pal than not be anything at all to him.

Roxanne sneaked out of the booth just behind them and walked quickly to the counter at the back. Frankie and Zack had each been too caught up in their separate juvenile crushes to notice that she'd been listening. Zack McGraw was really eating his heart out over Holly Daniels, huh? Interesting.

Zack McGraw and Holly Daniels . . . and Bart Einerson. That was the *really* interesting part. Einerson was a gorgeous hunk and the son of a congressman, and his snooty sister was a key member of the Kennedy crowd. Everyone knew about them. Could she somehow use what she'd just learned as a wedge to split the crowd open? Once she broke down their friendships and turned them on one another, she would have a chance to win the position she deserved. Right in the middle of everything, with all the important guys buzzing around her and all the girls off somewhere, eating their hearts out!

She smiled to herself as she recalled Holly and Zachary kissing in the shadows at the Valentine's Day Dance. What luck that she had wandered by at that moment! She was not quite sure what she was going to do with her information, but she had a strong feeling that she would find it very, very useful.

Chapter
6

On Saturday morning, Holly drove out to the Danberry Stable. She knew she would find Diana there. Maybe she could finally get her to talk — or at least listen. She had been trying ever since she spoke to Zachary, but Diana was deliberately, coldly avoiding her.

The day before, at lunchtime, Holly had made a point of taking the seat next to Diana, telling her that she needed to talk to her. Diana had given her a look that went right through her and said that she had to go to the library. Then Diana had gotten up and moved her tray to an empty table across the room.

Remembering that moment, Holly felt another flood of hurt and anger wash over her. Friends were people you knew you could trust, people you could count on to be loyal to you, take your side, and give you the benefit of the doubt. But

Diana wasn't acting the way a best friend ought to act. She wasn't acting like a friend at all.

Holly took a deep breath and told herself to calm down. She knew Diana was furious with her because Diana thought she had betrayed Bart. But every time Holly tried to talk to Diana, to tell her what had really happened, Diana seemed to become colder and more distant.

Holly sighed. Nothing was working out right. Whatever she did, she seemed to end up hurting people, even though she didn't mean to. She could still see the look on Zack's face when he had asked her if they could still be friends, and she had had to tell him no. He had looked so wounded that she'd wanted to put her arms around him. That would have been the worst possible thing to do, though. Instead, she had turned and walked away. He must have thought she was terribly cruel.

Holly was at a stoplight, and suddenly, someone honked behind her. She blinked. The light had changed. As she drove through the green light, a black Firebird pulled alongside. Through the tinted windows, Holly recognized three guys from the football team. The one by the window gestured and shouted something through the closed window. Then the car roared ahead, leaving a trail of gray exhaust. She shook her head. She didn't know whether they were trying to impress her or just stopping because they recognized Bart's girlfriend. Most guys on the team seemed to think any girl should be grateful for their attention.

Even Bart was like that sometimes. But Zack

wasn't. That was one of the things about Zack that had attracted Holly. He might be a star football player and all, but he had always been incredibly gentle and considerate with her. The day of the school ski trip, for instance, when he had found her stumbling around on the bunny slope, he'd stuck with her, taught her a few basics, and waited patiently when she goofed. Most guys wouldn't even have noticed what she was doing; they would have been too busy hotdogging around.

She shook her head again. This was no time to be thinking about Zack. It was over for good. Now what she had to do was convince Diana of that — before Diana felt it was her sisterly duty to inform Bart.

Diana's car was parked at the side of the stables, but she wasn't around. Irene Danberry, one of the owners, said Diana had taken a horse out about an hour before, and asked whether Holly wanted to take a horse and go find her. Holly wasn't much of a rider, so she declined and went outside to wait.

The air was chilly, but she found some bales of hay stacked in a sunny spot and stretched out on them. The warmth of the sun made her drowsy, and soon she felt her eyes closing. Gradually her thoughts drifted away from Diana and the stable.

A football game was going on, and Bart and Zachary were on opposite sides. Time after time they backed off, then charged head-on at each other. She kept shouting at them, begging them to stop, but they didn't pay any attention. Across the field, Diana, dressed as a pom-pom girl, cheered them on.

The crack of their two helmets split through the stands as the boys collided head to head. The two boys fell, and remained motionless on the muddy ground. She ran out to them, but when she finally managed to get their helmets off, she didn't recognize either of them. They were both complete strangers.

She opened her eyes with a start. Diana was at the edge of the clearing, on a bay horse, watching Holly with an expressionless face. For one crazy moment Holly wondered how Diana had managed to get out of her cheerleader costume and into boots and jeans so quickly. Then she remembered where she was, and why she had come.

"Hi," Holly called. She stood up and stretched.

Diana nodded silently and nudged the horse into a walk. Holly followed them across the stable yard and through the wide doorway of the barn, then stood by while Diana dismounted.

"Can I help?" Holly asked.

"No, thanks." Diana turned her back and began to unfasten the cinch that held the saddle on. The horse shifted restlessly, sidestepping away. "Whoah, girl," Diana said softly. The horse gave a snort and stood still.

Holly waited quietly while Diana put the saddle away and started wiping down the mare. She kept hoping that Diana would say something, anything, to break the silence that had stretched beyond awkward and was nearing the point of being unbearable. But Diana's lips were closed so tightly that they looked almost white.

"I tried to call you," Holly said timidly.

"Yeah," said Diana. "I know."

"When you didn't call back, I figured the only way I was going to get to talk to you was to come find you."

Diana was too involved in combing a knot out of the horse's mane to answer.

"Aren't you even going to listen?" Holly pleaded. "That's not very fair!"

Diana spun around. "Fair? That's a laugh! What about you? Were you being fair, sneaking around with some guy from Stevenson?"

"It wasn't like that, Di. That's what I've been trying to tell you."

"No?" She picked up a brush and turned her attention back to the horse. Over her shoulder she said, "It sure looked that way to me."

"If you'd just let me explain. . . ." Holly felt the tears gathering in her eyes, ready to overflow. She blinked them back.

"Look," she began, "I know I made a mistake. All I'm asking you to do is try to understand how it happened." She paused to study Diana's back, as if she could read her friend's reactions from it.

"No matter what you may think," Holly continued, "I never encouraged Zachary. I just didn't *dis*courage him enough. I don't know . . . he was very sweet, and a little lost from being transferred to Kennedy like that. And I guess I was feeling lonely, too. You know how hard I've been working, trying to get a scholarship. I've had practically no social life since September."

Her voice faltered. How long could she go on talking to somebody's back? But she had to make Diana see what had happened, *how* it had happened.

"I really missed Bart. I think something about Zack reminded me of him. . . . And Zack was so nice to me. I didn't see any harm in being friendly." She fell silent for a moment, then added, "I should have known that he was getting a crush on me, but I didn't."

Diana glanced over her shoulder. "I don't care about his crushes," she said. "What about yours?"

"Mine? I never. . . . Look, I *like* Zack. But that's all. I don't really have any romantic feelings about him. He's a very sweet guy, and I wish we could be friends. But the way he feels, the way things are, that's impossible. I see that now."

"Humph. Maybe you see it, but what about him?"

"I've told him that it is totally and completely over between us. I hope he can accept that. But whether he does or not, that's the way it is."

Diana turned around and for the first time looked directly at her. Her expression had softened. "Oh, Holly," she said, "I wish I could believe you. I *want* to believe you. I hate feeling so separate from you."

"Cross my heart," Holly said.

Diana had tears in her eyes, but she smiled at that childhood phrase. "You're such a goof sometimes," she said, reaching out to give Holly a hug. "How can I stay mad at you?"

Holly picked up a sponge and started helping Diana wipe down the horse. There was something else on her mind, something she had to ask Diana. Holly hoped she wouldn't ruin the good mood that had developed between them, but she had to take the chance. "About Bart," she said.

Diana gave her a shrewd look. "What about Bart?"

"Well, you know that ever since that whole silly business with Matt Jacobs last year, I've worried about doing anything that might get him jealous."

"You should have thought of that sooner," Diana said. "Still, I know he's kind of crazed in that department. I won't tell him about you and Zack, if that's what you're getting at. *But*" — Diana raised a warning finger — "if he gets wind of it from anyone else and asks me about it, I won't lie to him for you. I'll tell him what I know, and that includes what you've just told me. How he'd react, I don't know."

"I do," Holly said. "He'll do a good imitation of Mount St. Helens and blow his top. But it won't happen. Nobody thinks there was anything going on between me and Zachary."

"*I* thought so," Diana pointed out.

"I wanted to ask you about that. What made you think something was going on between me and Zachary? I tried so hard to hide it. Did someone say something to you?"

Diana's face closed down. "No one said anything," she replied. Her voice was cool again. "I saw for myself, at the dance. You were kissing, and I didn't see you struggling to get loose."

Holly winced, recalling the moment. "Oh, no, oh, Di — it must have looked so bad. When I got a piece of paper saying I had a computer Valentine, I couldn't resist finding out who the computer had matched me with. At first I was sure Bart had come home to surprise me, but then Zack was standing there waiting for me. And then things happened too fast. I don't know what came over me. I thought a couple of people might have walked by, but it was pretty dark. I figured they wouldn't notice or recognize us."

"*I* recognized you. It ruined the rest of the evening for me."

"I'm sorry. Did you tell anyone? Jeremy?"

"Of course not," Diana said soberly. "If I'd spread the news around, it would have hurt Bart as much as what you did."

"I said I'm sorry," Holly repeated, "and I am. And I don't want Bart to get hurt any more than you do."

"I know that," Diana said in a softer tone.

"Anyway, since the dance I've hardly even said hello to Zack. No one knows a thing. It was just pure bad luck that you saw us at the dance, and that kind of luck doesn't happen twice. If you keep it to yourself, it'll be as if it never happened. I wish it hadn't!"

"Too late for that," Diana said. "But at least we can make sure that things are over with Zachary, and that you and Bart have a fantastic time while he's in town."

"What day is he arriving? I'd like to come with you to the airport, if that's okay."

"Sure. He'll be coming in late Friday night. Hey — what's wrong?"

"The debate tournament," Holly wailed. "Down at the University of Virginia. It's next weekend! I have to be there from early Friday morning until Saturday night!"

"Don't worry, it'll work out," Diana said. "I'll drive down to UVA with Bart first thing Saturday morning, so you won't miss any of your time together. Besides, it'll be very interesting. He wouldn't want to pass up a chance to watch you argue with somebody else!"

"Very funny. I only wish I had the weekend totally free to spend with him. Still, he'll be staying through the next weekend, too, won't he?"

Diana nodded slowly. "I hate to mention it," she said, "but the following weekend is the Maple Sugarin' Festival at the Nature Center."

"That's right, you mentioned it to me a while back."

"I've been putting in a lot of work on it, trying to make it a success."

"Oh, it will be," Holly assured her friend.

"With any luck we'll be able to make it into an annual event," Diana continued. "But right now, not too many people know what it is or even know about it at all. And as head of the Kennedy Wilderness Club, I promised I'd get a lot of our students there. . . ." Her voice trailed off.

"Students like Holly Daniels and Bart Einerson?" Holly said with a grin.

"Among others," Diana said, returning the grin. "It really will be fun," she added anxiously. "You'll be able to watch them make maple syrup from the raw sap, and — "

"Okay, I'm sold," Holly said with a laugh. "But don't blame me if Bart wants to leave early and go for a drive."

"I won't. In fact, I might blame you if he *doesn't*!"

Diana's horse gave a whinny that sounded like agreement, and the two girls began to laugh. Holly was content; she had won her friend back again. Everything was back to normal.

Or almost everything. Holly only wished she could make sure Zack McGraw felt the same way.

Chapter 7

Matt Jacobs poured a glass of soda, filled a bowl with popcorn, and walked over to where Dee Patterson was sitting. She moved her camera to make room. "Good party," he said over the music.

She nodded and took a handful of popcorn. The front door opened and another bunch of people arrived. The Prestons' living room was filling up fast.

"Is Pamela coming?" asked Dee.

"I don't know."

Something in his tone made her look at him. His face was very still and controlled. She said carefully, "Someone told me that you and Pamela . . . uh, aren't seeing each other anymore . . . ?"

"Word travels fast, I see," he replied.

"Oh, I'm really sorry to hear that. Was it rough?"

He hesitated. "We didn't have a big fight or

anything. But we realized that we'd grown apart instead of together. We're still friends, but we're not a couple anymore."

"I'm sorry. It never feels good to break up, even when you both know it's the best thing to do."

"No, that's for sure." He took a long sip of his soda. "I'm just glad we were together as long as we were. It never really figured, somebody as talented and artistic as her going with a grease monkey like me."

"Matt Jacobs, you — "

He held up a hand to stop her. "Just kidding," he said. "What I really meant was that our interests are too different."

"That's better," Dee said. "I really hate to hear people putting themselves down. Pam likes to paint and you like to work on cars and I like to take pictures — "

"And Jonathan likes to organize worthwhile events," Matt added with a grin. "Have you noticed anything unusual about this party?"

"Well . . . I didn't hear about it until this afternoon. That's unusual."

"Yeah. He dreamed it up last night. What else?"

She looked around the room. "I see a lot of new faces. Is that what you mean?"

"Uh-huh."

"Who are they?" Dee asked. "Some of them look familiar, but. . . ."

Matt's grin broadened. "You've probably seen them in class or passed them in the halls."

"Kids from Stevenson?"

"Yup. Tonight is the kickoff of Jonathan's newest crusade, to make the Stevensonians into true-blue Cardinals."

"Matt," said Dee. "I hate to have to tell you this after four years at Kennedy, but Cardinals are red."

"Minor problem. You know what I mean. Anyway, Jonathan thinks we should do more to make the Stevenson kids feel welcome, so he decided to throw a party."

"That was a nice idea," Dee said. "I don't know if it will work, though."

"Why not?"

Dee waved her hand. "Look around the room. There's a clump of Stevenson kids over there by the popcorn and another group by the fireplace, and the rest of us are standing around talking to ourselves and ignoring them. You call that making them feel welcome?"

"Well. . . ."

Dee slung her camera around her neck and stood up. "Come on," she said.

"Where are we going?"

"Where do you think?" she said, taking his hand and pulling him to his feet. "We're going to enlist in Jonathan's crusade."

As she followed Roxanne up the walk, Frankie felt her stomach tying itself into knots. Walking into the sub shop, where she scarcely knew anyone was tough for her — but walking into a party at a stranger's house was even worse! She sighed. Would she ever have the kind of self-confidence Roxanne had? Being confident was probably

71

easier if you were gorgeous and smart, and had always known how to deal with boys — like Rox did.

"Come on, Frankie, you're not going to a funeral! This is a party. Look happy," Rox said as she put on a brilliant smile and gave the bell a long push.

Jonathan opened the door.

Roxanne said in a flirty voice, "Hello, Jonathan. Hope I'm not too late."

"Hi, Rox," he replied casually. "No, the party's just getting started. But I thought you weren't going to be able to come tonight."

"I changed my plans," Roxanne said. "I couldn't miss *your* party."

Frankie was amazed that Roxanne was even invited at *all*, after the Valentine's Day scam she played on Jonathan.

"Well, it's always good to see you, Rox," said Jonathan. Then he looked past her. "Hi, Frankie, nice to see you. Come on in."

The welcome made Frankie feel even shyer. She had really liked getting Jonathan's invitation, but the idea of having to talk and mingle at a big party full of kids she didn't know practically made her break out in a rash. She hadn't even been sure she would go, until Roxanne called to urge her and ask for a ride. But if Rox was going, that made it easier for Frankie. Hanging around at a party with someone she knew — especially Rox, who could soak up enough attention for two people — made her feel less awkward.

"Hi, Frankie," someone called from the living

room. It was Molly, who knew Frankie's little sister from the Fitness Center. Molly taught aikido, and Frankie's sister took gymnastics. Frankie glanced around to tell Roxanne she'd be back in a minute, but Rox was already heading toward a group of kids.

"Do you know these people?" Molly asked Frankie, and rattled off four or five names. "This is Frankie; she just transferred from Stevenson. She's the one who worked out the computer dating program for the dance," Molly explained to a group of Kennedy-ites.

"Really?" one guy said with a grin. "You owe me one. You know who I found when I went to my personal rendezvous? Your program had matched me up with my cousin! I guess we *are* a lot alike . . . but that wasn't much of a romantic surprise!"

Molly laughed. "Maybe you were disappointed, but think how bad *she* must have felt."

"It just shows you," someone added, "it's all relative."

The loud groans that greeted this remark drew over two or three others, including a boy Frankie remembered from English class back at Stevenson. He nodded and smiled. Soon eight or ten of them were standing in a loose circle, swapping jokes, rumors, and opinions about teachers, movies, records, and where in Rose Hill to get the best pizza. Frankie liked the feeling of being part of the group, and soon she found herself talking and laughing with the others.

She looked up and caught her breath. Zachary was standing in the doorway with Jonathan. He noticed her and gave her a friendly grin, but went on listening to Jonathan. Her hopes dimmed. Zack was glad to see her, but it was clear to her that he thought of her as a pal and nothing more.

Someone tapped Frankie on the arm. She blinked and looked around. The guy who had been computer-matched with his cousin said, "I'm getting more soda. Want some?"

"Oh. Thanks."

"Anyone else?" he said in a louder voice. Three or four cups were pushed toward him. He backed away in mock alarm.

"I'll come help you carry," Frankie said. As they walked across the room, Zack's eyes followed her. Did he seem disappointed? Had he been meaning to come talk to her and was sorry to see her walk away? She sighed as she walked to the food table. What an imagination you have, she told herself.

Zachary had come to the party hoping to see Holly. He knew she didn't want to talk to him, and he didn't have much hope she'd change her mind. Maybe he was being a fool, but he just wanted to see her — the way she looked and moved, the expression on her face.

While Jonathan kept him in the hallway, trying to talk intelligently about football, Zachary was scanning the crowded living room. There were lots of people, standing and sitting, and he couldn't see all of them, but he didn't see Holly anywhere.

Frankie was in the living room, though, in the middle of a group of people. She caught his eye and gave him a smile. He smiled back. He was glad to see that she was having such a good time. She deserved it, if anyone did. She was a really sweet kid and a good friend, someone he could turn to when he just had to talk about his troubles. She was the only one who knew about his feelings for Holly. What would he have done without the sympathy and understanding she gave him?

He nodded to a couple of guys who were standing with a bunch of other Stevenson kids. They didn't look very comfortable, and they weren't mixing with any of the Kennedy crowd. He knew that Roxanne was going around telling everybody that the Kennedy students were doing everything they could to exclude them. But Zack had known Roxanne long enough to know what she was like, and to know that he shouldn't believe everything she said. After all, Jonathan seemed like a nice guy, and he *had* invited a bunch of Stevenson kids to his party.

His thoughts wandered back to Holly. What if he had been going to Kennedy all along, instead of transferring in? Would that have made a difference in the way Holly looked at him? Maybe not. He still would have been just a jock, not part of her smart, confident crowd.

Jonathan was trying really hard to talk football, which he disliked along with every other contact sport. "I hear we've got a couple of sophomores coming up who'll make a real difference to our defensive line," he said.

His musings interrupted, Zachary looked at Jonathan blankly for a moment, then said, "Yeah, the coach thinks so. I don't know. I haven't seen them play yet."

Was Holly going to show up at the party at all? Maybe she was staying away because she knew he might be there. He didn't know what he had done that could make her dislike him that much. What Frankie had told him the other day had made sense when he heard it, but now he felt as confused as ever. Maybe it would help to talk to her again.

"I'm sorry I won't be around to see *you* play in a Cardinals uniform," Jonathan continued. "I'll never forget the job you did on us when we played Stevenson last fall — it was one of the few games I actually went to see!"

"Football's a team sport," Zachary said with a shrug. Frankie was walking off with some guy, and he wondered where they were going. "I was just part of the team."

Jonathan clapped him on the shoulder. "A quarterback? Part of the team, sure, but even I know enough about football to know you're the main man." The doorbell rang. "Oops, I'd better get that. I'll catch you later, okay, Zachary? Get yourself some food, enjoy the party."

"Sure, thanks."

Alone for a moment, Zack looked around. He hadn't checked out the room in back yet. There was music coming from that direction. Did Holly like music? He started down the hallway, shaking his head, as he realized he didn't even know *that* much about her.

* * *

Greg helped Katie down onto the couch, propped her crutches against the wall, and leaned closer. "How's that?" he asked. "Do you want a cushion under your foot?"

She shifted her weight to a more comfortable position. "I'm fine," she replied.

"Can I get you anything? How about some popcorn?"

"Sure," she said, "if you're having some."

"I'll be right back. Don't go away."

She smiled at the joke, but she didn't really think it was funny. She almost wished she *could* go away, to some place where she didn't have to watch all her friends dancing and doing all the things she couldn't do now. It was true, what people said — you never appreciate something until you have to do without it.

"Hi, Katie," Emily said, plopping down on the arm of the sofa. "How are you feeling?"

"I can't complain," she replied.

Emily gave her a disbelieving look. "Really. Why not? If I were you, I'd be complaining like mad!"

"I guess I mean I shouldn't complain."

"Oh? Who says? You mean if you do, all your friends will go off and say, 'That K.C.! Every time she breaks her leg, all she can do is complain!' "

A smile tugged at the corners of Katie's mouth. "Okay, then," she said, "you asked for it. My cast weighs a ton, my leg always itches in places I can't reach to scratch, I wake up whenever I try to turn over during the night, and I can't wait until I can throw those stupid crutches into the fireplace. And that's just for starters!"

"What does the doctor say?"

"I'll be getting a walking cast at the end of the week. How long that has to stay on depends on how fast the break mends. But it doesn't really matter. However quickly it mends, however hard I train to get back into shape, my chances of competing this spring are just about zero."

Greg returned carrying a cup of soda in each hand, and a big bowl of popcorn balanced on his forearms. "Help!" he said calmly. Emily grabbed the bowl of popcorn as it started to slide off his arm.

"Thanks, Em." He handed one of the cups to Katie and offered the other to Emily, who shook her head. "Has K.C. been telling you how much she's been enjoying her broken leg?" he asked.

Katie smiled. "Actually, she's been letting me cry on her shoulder."

"Good exercise," Greg said. "Speaking of exercise, did Katie tell you she's planning to be back in shape in time for the last gymnastics meet this spring?"

Katie caught Emily's eye and gave a little shake of her head. She could confide her doubts to someone like Em, but Greg was another matter. She didn't want to bring up her feelings of panic again after he'd been so supportive the last time they'd hashed this out.

"Really?" Em replied, looking from Katie to Greg. "That's great! But however long it takes, the important thing is to get over it completely.

Right, Katie? Oh, there's Elise — I've got to go talk to her before she takes off."

Katie waved good-bye to Emily and sat back to enjoy the party. Why didn't Greg sit down, too? He was standing next to the sofa, bouncing up and down as if his excess energy was about to bubble over.

"Hey," she called softly. But before she could finish, he said, "I'll be right back," and walked away.

Across the room, someone cranked up the volume on the stereo. Four or five couples started dancing. Katie watched and tried to put aside her feelings of envy. She was glad they could enjoy themselves, even if she couldn't join them. Suddenly she stiffened. One of the dancers was Roxanne Easton. Which guy was she trying to sink her claws into this time? Katie leaned her body one way, then the other, but she couldn't see.

Brian gave Karen a nudge with his elbow. "Over there," he said. "In the corner."

Karen looked over. Daniel Tackett was leaning against the wall, hands in the pockets of his jeans, watching the party with a superior smile on his face.

"Maybe now would be a good time to ask him to contribute to the paper," she said.

Brian tilted his head in Daniel's direction. "Go ahead. He looks as if he's waiting for something interesting to happen."

Karen straightened up and tossed her hair back over her shoulder. "I will."

Daniel seemed not to notice she was coming toward him until she stopped right in front of him.

"Hello," she said.

He nodded coolly.

"Nice party."

He looked away.

Karen felt the color rise in her cheeks, but she kept her voice casual. "I'm glad I ran into you. I read that issue of your paper that you gave me. I liked it."

"Did you?" He sounded disinterested, as if whether she liked it or not didn't concern him at all.

She plowed ahead. "Yes, I did. You printed a lot of good, gutsy stuff. *The Red and the Gold* could use more of that kind of journalism."

He met her eyes for the first time. She couldn't read the expression on his face. "I seem to remember saying something like that myself," he said. "I also remember that your friend, Conan the Barbarian over there, nearly kicked me out of your office for saying it."

"I'm sorry for the misunderstanding," Karen said calmly. Daniel snorted at her comment, but she continued. "It shouldn't have happened. What I'd like is to see if we can get past that. I'd like you to contribute to *The Red and the Gold*."

"Contribute what? An interview with the captain of the volleyball team?"

"Sure, if you think that will help make the paper into what you think it should be. Or anything else you want."

He straightened up and narrowed his eyes. "Anything?"

"I'm still the editor," Karen reminded him.

He leaned back again. "Right. I nearly forgot." He looked out into the room, as if she were already gone. Just as she was about to explode, he glanced over and said, "I'll think it over and let you know."

Thanks, she thought as she stalked away. Thanks a bunch!

Chapter
8

Brian tossed the copy of *The Stevenson Sentinel* on top of a stack of papers and stood up. "One-ten," he announced. "Do you think he'll show up?"

Karen looked up from the article she was working on. "Who knows? Maybe the big scoop he promised me wasn't so big after all. Anyway, after the other night, I don't much care," she said. "The paper's gotten along just fine without him, and it can go on doing so without him. He may be good, but that doesn't give him the right to treat people like dirt."

"Maybe it's partly my fault," said Brian. "If I hadn't lost it and practically thrown him out of the office. . . ."

"Maybe. But do you remember the way he walked in here before he even knew who we were?"

Brian laughed. "Coming to show the amateurs

how they do it in the big time. Okay, so Tackett is arrogant and conceited and tactless. Did I miss anything?"

"He also had some decent criticisms of the paper, and he may have some good ideas for improving it," said Karen.

"Right. And you know how to deal with constructive criticism and how to change what needs to be changed," Brian said. "That's why you asked Tackett to contribute to the paper. Right?"

"Right," said Karen in a gloomy voice. "Maybe he won't show up."

She returned to the article for a couple of minutes, while Brian paced the office restlessly. Suddenly she banged her pencil on the desk top. "I don't get it," she declared.

"What's that?"

"The way Daniel's going at this, bringing somebody here for *me* to interview. Why doesn't he do the interview himself?"

"I give up," said Brian. "Why not?"

Karen frowned. "He gave me some song and dance about how he's not on the staff of *The Red and the Gold*, so he shouldn't be writing for it. I told him we accept articles from anyone at Kennedy, but he said he didn't feel right about it."

"Humph. Could be he doesn't want his precious name associated with the paper until it's more like what he thinks it should be." He glanced at his wrist. "Well, like you said, maybe he won't show up."

The door opened.

The girl who was standing there, framed by

83

the doorway, looked like a big-eyed waif straight out of a painting in a sidewalk art show. Fluffy blonde hair, raggedly layered, framed a round face with small, delicate features. Her jeans had been washed almost white, and her bulky yellow sweater, the sleeves pushed up to the elbows, seemed about three sizes too big for her. She reminded Karen of a tall, lanky ten-year-old — until she looked at the girl's eyes. Her eyes were grown-up. There was a knowing, almost cynical quality in them, as if she had seen it all.

"Hi," Karen began, "can I — " She broke off as Daniel Tackett's face appeared over the girl's shoulder.

"Go on in," he told the girl in a voice that carried. "I don't *think* they bite."

Once inside, he said, "Lily, meet Karen Davis and Brian Pierson. Karen is the editor of *The Red and the Gold*, and Brian — "

"I recognize Brian's name," the girl said. "I eat lunch with him almost every day. Well . . . not with him, with his voice."

Brian gave her a small smile. "Another fan," he said.

"This is Lily Rorshack," Daniel continued. "She's a junior and another transfer student from Stevenson."

"Hi, Lily," said Karen. "Why don't we all sit down?" She and Brian pulled chairs into a circle.

"So," she said once they were settled, "I understand Daniel thinks I should interview you for the paper. Why is that?"

"Well, I — "

Daniel interrupted her. "Lily is going to be representing Kennedy High School this weekend at the invitational forensics tournament in Charlottesville."

"You mean the debate tournament?" Karen frowned. "I thought Greg Montgomery and Holly Daniels — "

"They're the Kennedy debate team, yeah," Daniel said. "Most people don't know there's anything to forensic meets except the debates. Actually, there are all kinds of speaking competitions at these meets. Lily here is competing in the improvisational speaking division of the tournament. She'll be doing a humorous monologue, and she has a very good chance of taking first place with it. On the other hand, from what I hear, Daniels and Montgomery will be lucky to make the finals."

Karen's frown deepened. "Let me see if I understand you," she said. "You want me to run an interview with Lily in the paper because she's representing the school at an important competition and stands a good chance of winning. Is that right?"

"Yep."

Karen leaned back and spoke to the ceiling. "That sounds like a pretty good idea to me. But I'm a little confused. Why do *you* think it's a good idea? That's exactly the kind of article you were criticizing the other day."

"I — "

"Hold on." She straightened up and aimed her index finger at him. "Last week you came in here

85

complaining about what a bland, gutless, *blah* newspaper we put out here. Maybe you can explain to me how interviewing Lily is hard-hitting journalism, and interviewing Greg Montgomery or asking Diana Einerson to talk about the Maple Sugarin' Festival isn't."

His smile was just a few degrees away from a sneer. "Why don't you wait and see?" he said. "When you're done, if you don't think I've given you a real story, I'll apologize."

Brian muttered something under his breath that sounded like, "That'll be the day!"

Karen nibbled at the eraser of her pencil for a few moments. She didn't like the look on Daniel's face — as if he were laughing at her inside. Was he challenging her? Or making fun of her? Maybe it didn't matter. Lily sounded worth interviewing, even if she didn't produce gritty, gutsy news. Daniel and his friends might not believe it, but she wanted to do whatever she could to get the kids from Stevenson more involved in school activities. A big story on one who already was involved would be a good place to begin.

"Okay." She reached over to her desk for a notebook and flipped it open to a blank page. "Well, Lily," she said, "why don't we start by finding out a little about you? How did you get interested in improvisational speaking?"

The girl shrugged. "It just happened," she said. "One day I realized that crying made my eye makeup run and laughing didn't. It was either stop crying and start laughing instead, or give up eye makeup. So I decided I'd better look at the funny side of things. But other people didn't always see the funny side, so I decided to show it to them."

"Is the funny side that easy to find?" asked Brian.

"No, but a public restroom isn't easy to find, either. If you need it badly enough, you keep looking."

Brian chuckled. "I guess you've got a point there," he said.

"Better there than on the top of my head."

One thing Karen had no use for, was a page full of wisecracks. She went back to Lily's first answer. "You said you took up humor to keep from crying. Were you doing a lot of crying back then?"

Out of the corner of her eye, she noticed Daniel settle back in his chair. She wondered if he knew what Lily was going to say.

"I cried a little," Lily said. "Not as much as I wanted to. My dad — my *real* dad — hated to hear kids cry. So we learned not to do it, no matter what."

Karen frowned. "I'm not really following you," she said.

"Good, I hate being followed too closely. Well, when my dad was a kid, he always dreamed of pitching in the major leagues. But then he got married, and we kids came along, so he ended up driving a delivery truck. But whenever he'd been out drinking, which was about three working nights out of five, he'd come home and try to live out his dream. If he couldn't pitch for the majors, he'd pitch *at* the minors — me and my brothers."

"He'd throw things at you?"

"You bet. Plates, empty bottles — not full ones, but those never lasted long around him anyway — books. . . ." She reached up and brushed her hair away from her left temple. "It doesn't show up as much as it used to, but I call this my *Webster's Dictionary* scar. Maybe somebody once told Dad you had to pound knowledge into kids' heads, and he didn't quite understand what they meant."

"That's terrible," Karen exclaimed.

Lily gave her an odd, somehow chilling smile. "It's not so bad once you know how to duck. Timmy never did learn, poor kid. He's my little brother. He was about seven when Dad scored a direct hit with an empty Night Train bottle. Timmy's been pretty slow ever since. I guess you could say that after the Train hit him, he missed the boat."

"But — " Brian shook his head slowly. "Didn't anybody try to stop your father? Report him to the cops or something?"

"Who? Us kids? We thought everybody lived like that. My mom? Most of the time, she was too far out in the twinkie zone to know what year it was. Then one day Dad drove his van into a utility pole at sixty miles an hour. The insurance paid for a fantastic funeral. What a party that was! Afterward, we kept wondering how we could manage to have another one."

Karen was astonished by Lily's story, but she

kept fighting to keep her objectivity as a reporter. "Then your father was an alcoholic? And your mother was mentally ill?"

"Uh-huh," Lily said. "She would take a drink, too, now and then. Just to be sociable, you understand, but after Daddy died she really got into being sociable — with a whole string of different boyfriends."

"With parents like that, did you ever worry that problems like that might run in your family?"

Lily laughed. "A lot of things run in my family," she said. "Especially me!"

"How do you mean?"

"The day after I turned twelve, Mom's latest boyfriend asked me for a date. I didn't think I was old enough to date, so instead, I ran away. I kept running for a couple of years. The original marathon woman, that's me."

"But how did you live?" asked Brian. He was staring at her with a look of wonder on his face.

"Sometimes it didn't feel as if I *was* living," she replied in an offhand manner. "But I got by. I even made a few friends. Then I started hanging out with the wrong crowd. Funny thing — once I started ripping off everybody I knew so I could get by, nobody wanted to know me anymore."

"You were on your own from the time you were twelve," Karen repeated, "and you got . . . in trouble too, right?"

"Oh yeah. Hanging out all day gets to be boring, you know? So you make your own excitement. It's like Russian roulette, though. Sometimes you get caught; sometimes you don't. And before you know it, you've gotten old, and you're not even fourteen."

"So what happened?" Brian asked gently. "What turned it around for you?"

Lily shook her head. "If I knew for sure, I'd bottle it and get rich," she said. "Maybe it was humor that did it. I always liked to tell funny stories to make people laugh. After getting busted a few times, things weren't funny anymore, not even to me. And the people I was hanging with were so wild and reckless that they wouldn't have known a terrific story if it ran over and bit them on the leg."

She paused, then gave a sudden smile. "You could say the way I got my act together was by putting my act together. Somebody told me about a halfway house in Georgetown, and one day when I had nothing to do I dropped by. This guy and I talked for an hour, maybe more. I bounced lines off him, and I could see he thought I was funny, but he kept turning serious on me. Finally he asked me what my wildest dream was. Do you know what I told him?"

Karen was too wrapped up in her story to do more than shake her head.

"I said I wanted to do my act on Johnny Carson. And do you know what he said to me? He said, 'If you want to be a top banana, you've got to start at the bottom of the bunch!' "

She noticed their puzzled looks. "Top banana is what they called a star comedian in the old days," she explained. "What he meant was, if I wanted my dream to be anything more than a dream, I had to work hard for it. Get off the street, go back to school, take all the speech and English and history and social studies courses I could handle, and work on my act. That's what it's all for: my act.

"Sometimes I thought I wasn't going to make it," she continued. "Too often it seemed like I was trying to walk up the down escalator — I never got anywhere. Finally I got tired of trying to figure out the escalators, and took the elevator."

Brian suppressed a small smile.

"Anyway, at Stevenson I discovered dramatic interpretation and improvisational speaking. I started working with the speech coach there, and participating in forensics meets, and there I was. I mean, here I am. Well, both, I guess, because I *was* there and I *am* here. That's all."

She gave them both her pixie smile and sat back.

"And next weekend she just may win a trophy," Daniel said.

Karen looked over at Brian. He seemed as stunned by Lily's story as she was. It wasn't any particular detail that was so remarkably unusual, but the story as a whole and the way she told it, with that touch of humor that somehow made it more serious.

Every kid at Kennedy who had a problem with family, friends, the law, or just coping with life would relate to this girl. An article about Lily and the way she had triumphed over her background might even be an inspiration to a lot of people. And it would certainly have more pizzazz than the student council minutes or a splash-by-splash account of the swim team's latest outing.

Karen cleared her throat. "I'd like to write up this interview," she said. "This week's issue has already been sent to the printer, but the story can appear next week, along with an account of the tournament at Charlottesville. Whatever happens there, Lily, whether you win or not, is still newsworthy in my book."

"I agree," said Brian. "And I'd like to bring you over to the WKND studio in the next day or two, to get you to repeat some of what you just told us in front of the microphone. I can run the interview next week during my lunchtime show."

"Well, Lily?" Daniel added.

"I'd better go," she said, standing up. "I've got to prepare for the tournament."

"Great," Karen said. "Good luck. And Daniel . . . thanks for bringing Lily to meet us. I'll remember this afternoon."

"So will I," Daniel replied, with a broad smile. "Maybe Lily's story would even improve relations between rival newspaper editors."

The door closed.

"Whew!" Brian shook his head. "It really makes you wonder, doesn't it?"

"It certainly does," said Karen somberly. "Would I have had the strength to come through what she's come through? I really don't know."

"I don't, either. I'll tell you something else, though. When we go down to Charlottesville early on Friday, I'm not going to spend much time covering the debates. The real story is going to be at the improv sessions."

"That's funny," Karen said. "I was going to say the same thing."

"That *is* funny," Brian responded. "Now let's hope that, come Friday, Lily Rorshack is funny, too."

Chapter
9

It was quite a room, Holly told herself for the dozenth time. The gleaming wood paneling on the walls and the sparkling chandelier that hung from the center of the ceiling made it seem more like her idea of a courtroom than a schoolroom. But of course the University of Virginia wasn't just a school. It was a college, one of the oldest and most prestigious colleges in the East.

She snapped back to attention as the judge collected his notes and walked up to the podium. Holly was trying to appear calm and confident, but she was clutching her pen so tightly that her hand ached. She met Greg's eye for a moment and gave him a quick, sympathetic smile. He replied with a surreptitious thumbs-up.

They had won their first debate that morning, but she wasn't sure how to interpret their victory. The team from Tidewater High School in Virginia hadn't seemed as well prepared or as fast on their feet as they should have been. The judge devoted most of his comments after the debate to explaining why they had lost, rather than saying why Kennedy had won.

The second round had been a more even match. The team from Maryville Prep had obviously sent someone to scout their earlier debate, just as Kennedy had sent a guy to scout the Maryville Prep team. As a result, both sides were better prepared to match the other team's style of debate.

The judge had finished his initial comments and was beginning to review the course of the debate. "The affirmative presented three benefits to its plan," he said. "First, an oil import tax would provide an economic incentive for energy conservation. . . ."

Holly listened with half an ear. She knew the arguments that she and Greg had used by heart. She drifted off, reviewing in her own mind the speeches she had made. But Holly was all ears when the judge prepared to announce his decision.

"The affirmative's plan was demonstrated to be better than present policy," he announced. "Since the affirmative met its burden of proof, I award the decision to the affirmative."

The spectators applauded. *We won*, Holly thought exuberantly. She gave Greg a quick hug, then shook hands with the two kids from Maryville Prep. As she was putting her notecards back in her bag, Ms. Woodbury, the Kennedy debate coach, came over.

"Well done, you two," she said with a smile. "I

thought you would want to know that Tidewater just won its second-round debate."

Holly flashed a triumphant grin at Greg, who returned it. Under the complicated scoring system used at the tournament, the Kennedy team received extra points every time a team they had beaten won against someone else. Even if she and Greg lost their two remaining preliminary rounds, they could still make it into the finals if either Tidewater or Maryville Prep scored another victory.

"Round three doesn't start until four-thirty," Ms. Woodbury continued. "Why don't you take some time to relax and look around. We can meet again at a quarter to four to go over our strategy and polish a few arguments."

Greg waited patiently while Holly changed her black high-heeled pumps for a battered pair of white hightops. They didn't look quite right with her navy blue suit, white blouse, and borrowed pearls, but at least she would be able to stroll around the campus without getting stuck in the cracks in the sidewalk.

"This tie is going to strangle me," Greg remarked. He tugged at the collar of his shirt.

"Take it off," Holly suggested. In his three-piece suit and well-polished wingtip shoes he certainly didn't look like the usual Greg Montgomery, but she thought he looked quite distinguished.

Greg loosened the tie with a sigh of relief.

"When is K.C. coming down?" she asked him.

"This evening, with Brian and Karen. I hope

they make it in time for the evening round. It'll be nice to see some familiar faces in the audience."

"It sure will," Holly said with a faraway smile. Where was Bart now? Still in Montana? In the air already? She would have loved to be waiting for him at the airport, but the knowledge that she would see him the next morning — and then all of next week — almost made up for her disappointment.

At the door, Greg paused and looked in both directions. "I think I'll go hunt up a snack," he said. "What about you?"

"We just had lunch!" she laughed. "Not for me, thanks."

"You need to keep up your strength, you know. Arguing a case is strenuous work."

"It's not my strength that worries me," she joked. "It's my waist that I have to be concerned with. As a matter of fact, I think what's called for is a brisk walk across campus."

"I'd join you," he said, "but I feel as if I haven't eaten in three weeks."

Holly reached up to pat him mockingly on the shoulder. "Don't worry, Montgomery." She pointed to the left. "I think the cafeteria is down that way. And I hear a piece of chocolate cake calling your name," she said, smiling.

"Food!" he croaked and took off. "See you later," he added over his shoulder.

Holly turned the other way and took the first set of doors that led outside. Across the road, a willow tree wore a faint, almost undetectable haze of green. The other trees were still bare, but they too seemed somehow expectant, as if aware that spring was about to transform them. She stopped long enough to put on her jacket, then walked up the path toward a set of low red brick buildings.

After a few steps she stopped, entranced. Two long, columned buildings faced each other across a courtyard. At the far end, closing off and completing the vista, wide steps led up to the pillared porch of a huge dome-topped building that looked like something built during the Roman Empire.

"Pretty impressive, isn't it?" a voice said. "You're here for the forensics tournament, right?"

She looked around, then nodded. A boy with dark hair was smiling at her. His jeans and Scandinavian sweater made it apparent that he was not one of the debaters, who were all dressed for success in suits and dresses.

"What you're looking at is the original campus of the university," he continued. "Designed by Jefferson and built in the eighteen-twenties."

"You mean Thomas Jefferson?" she said. "The president?"

"Yup. He was quite a guy. He designed his own house at Monticello, too, but if you ask me, this was his masterpiece. The two long buildings were meant to provide housing for ten professors and two hundred students, as well as classrooms and dining halls."

"You seem to know a lot about it," Holly said. "Are you a student here?"

"Yup. This is my first year. My name's Bo Randolph."

"I'm Holly Daniels. How did you know I was a debater?"

"I could say it's your earnest look," he replied, "but the truth is, I'm a member of the student guide service that gives tours of the campus. We're always told in advance which groups are going to be arriving, and you're a little too short to be a member of the North Carolina men's basketball team. Would you like to take a look at the rotunda? It's fantastic, the way Jefferson fit three beautiful oval rooms into a circular plan."

Holly glanced quickly at her watch. It was just three-fifteen. "Why, yes," she said. "I'd like that."

Katie's doctor had her office in a small shopping plaza on the north side of town. After her appointment, Katie went outside and sat on a wooden park bench to wait for Karen to come pick her up. She propped her crutches against a nearby tree and tried to forget their existence. She hated those crutches. They were ugly and awkward, and at the end of the day her arms were sore from using them. Even more, she hated what they stood for in her mind: a reminder of her helplessness.

When the doctor had told her she was ready for a walking cast, she had hoped she could finally do without the crutches. Wasn't that what a walking cast meant? But when the doctor cut away the full cast, she was stunned to see how much her leg muscles had withered. Where had they gone? Could all her years of constant training and exercise vanish just like that, after only a few weeks in a cast? The doctor had told her that without use, her muscles would become significantly weaker, but Katie hadn't realized just what that would mean.

The walking cast was a big improvement, lighter and more maneuverable, but when she had stood up and tried to walk, she had almost fallen over. Her leg wasn't strong enough to support her weight. The doctor had told her for the thirty-eighth time not to worry, that her strength would gradually come back. Katie even half-believed her. But that wasn't the issue. She wanted her strength back *right now*.

A huge black motorcycle turned into the parking lot and slowed to a crawl. She glanced up. The guy on it was staring openly at her. He looked pretty creepy in his tattered jeans, beat-up leather jacket, and black leather gloves with the fingers cut away. As he passed, he gunned the engine and made the rear tire squeal. She looked away.

Out of the corner of her eye, she saw him pull over to the curb about a hundred feet down. She figured he was going to The Hall of Shame. That wasn't really its name, of course. The sign over the door of the notorious punk club read "Hall of Fame." But no one, not even the bunch of losers who hung out there, called it anything but The Hall of Shame.

As the biker opened the door of the club, the music, suddenly loud beyond endurance, blasted into Katie's brain. The door closed again and the noise faded, but it left her with a headache that pulsed along to the beat that she could still hear in the parking lot. She checked her watch. Karen had said she would pick her up at four-thirty. So far she was five minutes late.

Katie frowned and pushed her hands deeper into the pockets of her jacket. She didn't really mind that Karen was late. In fact, she had to admit that she wouldn't mind if Karen didn't come at all. Why go down to Charlottesville anyway? To watch Greg and Holly compete in the tournament? Compete, and maybe win? To hang out with Karen and Brian and listen to them go on about how well the newspaper and the radio station were doing, and how great it was that they had both been admitted to Brown? Of course she was happy for their successes; they were her friends. But she didn't want to spend the weekend in the company of so many winners, because she didn't feel like a winner anymore.

What would she say if someone at Charlottesville asked her who she was? A few weeks earlier, she wouldn't have thought twice. "I'm Katie Crawford. I'm a gymnast."

But now? What *could* she say? I used to be a gymnast? I'm a gymnast with a broken leg? Ridiculous! Her competitive instincts, and her conviction that she had to be a winner were as strong as ever, but *she* wasn't. She was as weak and helpless as a day-old kitten, and without her strength and agility, she didn't feel she was the same person.

What was the weekend going to be like for her? She and Karen and Molly were all supposed to be camping out in Sasha Jenkins' dorm room. Sasha had graduated from Kennedy the year before and was now a freshman at UVA. Would she be sleeping, broken leg and all, on the floor? Or would Sasha feel sorry for her and give Katie her bed? How would she get around? For all she knew, Sasha's room was up four flights of stairs!

101

She imagined herself clumping around a strange building in the middle of the night, trying to find the bathroom.

Greg and the others would help as much as they could, of course. She knew she could count on them. But she didn't want to be in a position where she *had* to count on them. Her presence would only be hassle after hassle for them. They might not admit it, even to themselves, but if she stayed away it would be a big relief to everyone. Greg could concentrate on his debating, and Karen and Brian could concentrate on their reporting, instead of worrying about her all the time.

A car horn tooted, and Brian pulled up at the curb. Karen and Molly waved excitedly, and Brian got out to help Katie in.

"Hey," he said, "I got a call from Greg just before I left the station. He and Holly won their first two debates. They're practically certain to be in the finals tomorrow."

"That's great," Katie said listlessly.

"And I talked to Sasha last night," Karen added as she opened the door on her side. "She's promised to show me around the student newspaper office and introduce me to some of the people who run it."

"Great," Katie said again.

"You know," said Molly, "Sasha knows a lot of different people on campus, from working on the paper. I bet she could take you to meet some of the gymnasts while we're there."

Katie had suddenly come to a decision. "That'd be great," she said. "The thing is, I can't go."

"Can't go?" Molly said.

Brian frowned. "What do you mean? You're not coming?"

"Uh-uh. I'm sorry, I would have called you, but I couldn't. I've got too much homework to do and I can't spare the time."

"But — " Karen began.

Molly interrupted her. "Listen, K.C., why don't you come down with us this afternoon, and then come back with me on the train tomorrow morning?"

"I couldn't — "

"I have to come back anyway," Molly continued. "Ted's coming home for spring break. How much homework are you going to do tonight, anyway?"

"It's not just that," Katie said. "The fact is, I feel worn out." She struggled to her feet and reached for the crutches. "All I want to do is go home and rest."

"Well. . . ." Brian studied her face. "Okay, if that's what you really want. Want us to drop you off at home?"

She shook her head. "My mom's already on her way," she lied. "You get going. You don't want to miss this evening's debate. You'll explain to Greg, won't you?"

"Sure, K.C.," said Brian. He started to say something else, then changed his mind. "Well, you take care of yourself. Get some rest, okay? We'll see you on Monday."

She watched the car pull away, then limped over to the telephone booth to call her mother. She had to pass the door to The Hall of Shame.

Three grungy-looking kids, two guys and a girl, were leaning against the wall, staring blankly into the parking lot. They looked totally spaced and wasted, but she suddenly felt that she had more in common with them, the losers of the world, than with Greg and her other overachieving friends. The thought chilled her, but somehow it was a comfort as well. At least she knew where she belonged. And that was the scariest part of all.

Chapter
10

Holly opened her eyes and looked up. During the night someone had changed everything about her room — the color of the ceiling, the feel of the bed, even the position of the window and door. How? Why? She closed her eyes, scrunched up her face, and tried to think. Then she remembered. She was in Charlottesville, in a dorm room, and the breathing from the other side of the room belonged to a UVA freshman who had offered to let a debater stay in her room for the weekend.

Keeping her eyes closed, she rolled onto her side and tried to convince herself that she was going back to sleep. It didn't work. Her mind refused to cooperate, insisting on replaying the highlights of the previous day's debates. She and Greg had been awarded the decision three times out of four. That was a remarkable performance, considering how few competitions they had entered up until now. It meant that they were one of the eight teams in today's elimination rounds.

She knew that today was going to be a very different experience, though. The team that had beaten them on Friday afternoon was a real powerhouse. Rittenhouse High, from Pennsylvania, had taken their regional championship several years in a row and done well in national competition. She and Greg had found themselves totally outclassed, like schoolyard soccer players thrust into the World Cup finals. The judge did make a point of mentioning their admirable fighting spirit, though, just before knocking down all their important arguments.

What did it really matter how they did? Why did she care so much? Holly didn't really even like debating — she'd admitted that to herself long ago. And besides, she was going to see Bart this morning for the first time in many weeks. That was much more important to her than any debate competition. But suddenly she began to see that Bart was part of the reason she was so concerned about the tournament. She wanted him to see her doing something difficult, and doing it well. It didn't have to be debating — that was almost unimportant. It could just as well have been volleyball or needlepoint or tuning a carburetor.

She wanted him to be proud of her. That was the real point. She wanted to see the look in his eyes when the judge praised her presentation in front of everyone. She wanted him to turn to the person in the next seat and say, "That's my girlfriend up there!" She wanted him to run up onto the platform afterward and give her a big hug, then stand there beaming, with his arm around

106

her, while she accepted the judge's congratulations.

She sighed as she imagined the scene. Afterward, they would go somewhere more private and he would tell her how proud he had felt. She would tell him how much seeing his face in the audience had inspired her. They would confess how much they had missed each other, how lonely they had felt, and they would fall into each other's arms.

She sighed again, then reluctantly stopped hugging the pillow and opened her eyes. A soft gray light was spreading across the ceiling from the window. It must still be early, but she couldn't stay in bed any longer. She got up, as quietly as the squeaky bedsprings would allow, and slipped on her clothes.

"Mmph?" Holly's roommate said sleepily from the other bed. "What time is it?"

"It's early," Holly said softly. "Go back to sleep."

Outside, the rising sun was just beginning to dispel the nighttime chill from the air. A single bird gave a couple of tentative chirps, then let loose a whole series of trills. Holly stood taller and took a deep breath. Tournament or no tournament, this was going to be a beautiful day.

She walked with no particular destination in mind, turning down the first tree-lined street she came to. This weekend was teaching her something important, she realized. She was away from home and familiar surroundings, at an elegant, almost awe-inspiring college campus filled with strangers, and she was engaged in high-pressure competition. At another time in her life, that combination might have been too much for her to handle. Even now it was certainly scary. But the surprising thing was that she was handling it. She was even enjoying it — well, parts of it.

Ever since September, when Bart went back to Montana to go to college, Holly's thoughts had been bouncing back and forth between hope and fear. Her hope was to go to college with Bart, and her fear was that her grades wouldn't be high enough to get her a scholarship. Unless she won a scholarship to the University of Montana, she would have to go somewhere less expensive and closer to home, separated from Bart and from all her friends. Every time she had imagined that possibility, she had been sure she would never be able to bear it.

This morning, as she walked through the quiet streets of Charlottesville, she was beginning to think that she just might be able to face going to college on her own. Of course she'd have to cope with a new environment, but so would practically all of her classmates. And she would probably feel shy at first, but so what? Lots of people felt shy. Maybe once she was there she could organize a Shy People's Club!

Her stomach was telling her that it was past her breakfast time. For one scary moment she was sure that she had gotten herself hopelessly lost. She would never find her way back in time for the morning round of debates, never mind breakfast. Kennedy would be eliminated from the finals by default, Bart would go back to Rose Hill in disgust, and Greg and the others would never forgive her.

Holly took a deep breath. A couple of houses down the block, a woman in a bathrobe had come out on her front porch to get the morning paper. Holly called to her and asked for directions, and within five minutes she was back on the main street. She could see the campus a block away.

As she turned up the driveway, somebody called her name. She looked back. Diana was waving from the window of her car, and opening the door on the driver's side was —

"Bart!" she exclaimed.

Laughing, close to weeping, she ran over and flung herself into his waiting arms. He lifted her off the ground and swung her around.

"Hey," she protested. "I still need to breathe!"

"Want me to let go?" he teased.

"Uh-uh. Never." She rested her cheek against his chest. Being in his arms felt so familiar, so right. Sure, it was good to know that she could manage going off to college on her own, away from him; but she also knew that what counted was that they loved each other and wanted to be together.

"Hey, Holly," Diana called. "I don't want to interrupt anything, but have you had breakfast yet?"

She laughed. "Not at all. What about you?"

"Are you kidding? Bart got me up before the sun rose this morning to drive down here. You don't think he was going to let something as unimportant as breakfast slow us down, do you?"

Holly leaned back and smiled up at Bart. "Are you hungry?"

"Well — " He dropped into an exaggerated western drawl. "Now that you mention it, little lady, I reckon I could handle some grub. What do you say?"

"I'll leave the grubs to the robins, thanks! But I wouldn't mind some real food."

"We passed a pancake place on the way into town," Diana said. "How does that sound?"

After breakfast, Diana dropped Holly and Bart off near the campus and drove away to find Sasha's dorm. There was a little time before the morning debates, so they wandered hand in hand through a parklike area of woods and tiny clearings. Eventually they found a stone bench on the bank of a narrow stream to sit down on.

"Miss me?" Bart asked softly.

She nodded.

"Me, too," he said. "I spend so much time thinking of you that I don't even remember how to flirt."

"Do you remember how to kiss?" she asked teasingly.

"I don't know. Let's find out."

His lips met hers in a kiss so powerful, so sweet, that she almost forgot to breathe. On and on it went, until she felt everything else slipping away from her, leaving only the touch of Bart's lips and the pressure of his arms.

She completely lost track of the time until suddenly, Holly caught a glimpse of Bart's wristwatch. She let out a gasp. "I have to go," she cried. "I'll be late!"

"Okay," Bart said easily. "Come on, I'll walk you over."

They stopped at the dorm so Holly could change from her jeans into a green wool skirt, white blouse, and a soft green and white angora vest, and then headed across the campus. As they neared the building where the morning debates would take place, someone said, "Hi, Holly. Good luck today."

She glanced around and waved. "Thanks, Bo," she replied.

"Who was that guy?" asked Bart after they passed him.

"Bo? He's a freshman here. I met him yesterday. He's a member of the student guide service, and he gave me a tour of the campus."

"Really? That must have been fun."

She glanced at him uncertainly. Was he being sincere or sarcastic? Once she had known his every mood and tone of voice, but after being away from each other so long he seemed almost like a stranger. He couldn't really be jealous of a casual acquaintance like Bo, could he? Not after their morning together. Surely he must be feeling the same thing she was — the delight of being with each other again; the warm, wonderful knowledge that they belonged together. Of course he was. It was silly to worry about something like that.

As they walked up the steps, she took his arm and sighed to herself. All she needed now to complete her happiness was a letter of acceptance from the University of Montana.

Roxanne stopped at the spot where two paths crossed and looked around. A great-looking guy in a varsity sweater was coming along one of the walks.

"Excuse me," she said in a honey-sweet voice, "but do you think you could help me?"

"I can try," he said. "What's the problem?"

"I'm looking for the forensics tournament, and I'm afraid I've gotten myself lost."

"You're practically there," he said. "That's the entrance over on the left. Someone inside can tell you what room you want."

"Thank you, you're very kind." She would have smiled and tried to continue the conversation with him, but he was already on his way again.

As she walked up the steps, she wondered if making the trip down had been a mistake. She had about as much interest in debating as she did in beekeeping. Still, for whatever reason, the crowd at Kennedy had decided that this was the place to be this weekend. For Roxanne, that was reason enough to come, but she also knew that Greg Montgomery was one of the debaters. She wondered if he had driven down in that luscious Mercedes he had. As an afterthought, she wondered if he had brought Katie Crawford with him. Not that it mattered too much. By now he must be getting bored playing nursemaid to his girlfriend.

In the hallway, she waved and smiled to a small group of Kennedy students. They didn't act as if they were very glad to see her, but she didn't care. The important thing was that they had seen her. They'd change their attitudes before long, when they realized what a dangerous enemy she could be.

A tall, slim boy in an elegantly tailored tweed jacket filled her in on what was happening. The Kennedy debate team had won their first elimination round that morning, then had the bad luck to draw the best team in the tournament on the second round. Holly and Greg had presented some strong arguments, and though they had lost, it had been a close decision. Now they were about to compete in the consolation round to decide whether they took third or fourth place.

As she was talking to him, she noticed Zachary enter the auditorium. What was *he* doing there? Her eyes narrowed. She had a sudden hunch that this trip might turn out better than she had thought. She thanked the boy in the tweed jacket and went in. The debaters were already at their desks on the platform. She caught Greg's eye and waved. He nodded coolly and continued to study his notes. Holly Daniels stared right through her.

She scanned the audience. She didn't see Katie anywhere. That brought a satisfied smile to her lips. There was always some kind of party after these interschool events, and it looked as if Greg would be going to it dateless. If she had anything to do with it, he wouldn't stay that way for long.

Her gaze fastened on a big, ruggedly handsome guy sitting by himself in the seventh row. She knew she'd seen him somewhere before. Who was he? After a few moments of concentration, it came to her: He was Diana Einerson's brother, the one who was supposed to be Holly Daniels' boyfriend. She remembered him from a party after a Stevenson-Kennedy game the year before. What was his name, Burt? No, Bart. Aha! she thought. Bart . . . Holly . . . and Zack. Hmm. . . .

She strolled over and casually sat down in the seat next to his. He barely glanced at her. All his attention was focused on the platform. She waited a moment, just long enough to make it seem as if she had sat down next to him purely by accident, and then said, "Excuse me, didn't you go to Kennedy High, in Rose Hill?"

He looked at her again. This time he smiled. "That's right. I don't think I remember you, though."

"Oh, I wasn't at Kennedy when you were. I'm there now, though. My name's Roxanne Easton."

"Hi, Roxanne. I'm Bart Einerson."

"Hi. Are you off at college now?"

He grinned. "Can't you tell? Yeah, I'm at the University of Montana."

"Really? How fascinating! I've never been west of Chicago. I'd love to hear all about it."

"Don't get me started," he joked. "I can talk all night."

She raised an eyebrow and smiled. After a short pause, she said, "I guess you've heard about all the changes at Kennedy since you graduated. I was one of the people who was transferred when they closed Stevenson High."

"I heard about that," Bart said. He was beginning to sound a little bored.

Roxanne rushed ahead. "It hasn't been that easy, moving to a new school in the middle of the year. Most of the Stevenson kids have had a hard time getting to know the kids at Kennedy, and to tell you the truth, we haven't gotten the greatest welcome from a lot of people."

The moderator tapped the microphone on the podium.

"Too bad," said Bart. "Look, I think they're starting." He turned to face the platform.

It was now or never. "There have been some exceptions, of course. You know Holly Daniels, don't you? The girl up there?" He turned back to face her. She had his full attention now. "She and Zachary McGraw have gotten *very* close, if you know what I mean. He used to be Stevenson's star quarterback."

Bart had gone pale. "What are you talking about?" he demanded. "And what do you want from me? How do *you* know all this?"

"Oh, everybody knows. They're very open about it. Why, at the Valentine's Day Dance I happened to walk past while they were kissing each other. They didn't notice me, of course, but it looked very romantic. Oh, look," she added, "that's Zack sitting right over there. He can't keep his eyes off her, can he? Isn't that sweet?"

Bart looked in the direction she was pointing. Then, without a word, he stood up and walked away. Roxanne wondered if he was going to pick a fight with Zachary, but instead he went over to his sister, took the seat next to her, and began to talk urgently in an undertone. At one point Diana looked up and glared at Roxanne. She gave her an innocent smile in return, then sat back to enjoy the debate.

Holly let her eyes sweep across the rows of spectators. "In conclusion, ladies and gentlemen," she said in a confident voice, "the objections raised by the speakers for the negative are either illogical, irrelevant, or against the weight of the evidence. We have shown that our plan for a federal tax on imported oil is necessary, effective, and practical, and we therefore urge you to award the decision to the affirmative. Thank you."

The applause was loud in her ears as she walked back to the table and sat down. "Great job!" Greg whispered.

"You, too," she replied. "Shh!" The judge was coming up to the platform. She closed her eyes for an instant. Whatever the decision, she couldn't do anything to affect it now. Opening her eyes again, she looked out into the audience and caught Bart's eye. He and Diana were sitting in the middle of a row of seats about halfway back. He was too far away for her to read his expression, but she could sense that he was watching her. Whether the judge agreed or not, she felt she had spoken and argued very well in the debate. Did Bart think so, too? Was he feeling as proud of her as she had hoped he would? She would know in a few minutes.

The judge spoke at length, analyzing each side's arguments, evidence, and counter-arguments. Clearly he had thought it was a very close contest.

That was bad news. The rule in debating was that the side taking the affirmative, her side, bore the burden of proof; that is, Holly and Greg needed to show there were very good reasons why there should be a federal tax on imported oil. If the judge wasn't quite convinced by their case, or if he found the two sides evenly balanced, the negative won.

Suddenly Holly stopped taking notes and looked over at Greg. He was grinning broadly. So he had sensed it, too: the judge's comments were swinging over into their favor.

". . . And therefore I award the decision to the affirmative. And my congratulations to the members of both teams for an exciting and educational debate."

They had won! The debate was theirs, and so was third place in the whole tournament!

As the audience burst into applause, Holly jumped up, gave Greg an excited hug, and went with him to the center of the stage to shake hands with the judge and the members of the other team. She looked out into the auditorium. Diana and Bart had just managed to squeeze past the others in their row and were starting down the aisle to the platform. She smiled and raised her hand to wave to them.

Suddenly someone grabbed her and lifted her into the air. "What . . . ?" she gasped.

"Holly, you were great!" Zack exclaimed. "I never knew you could speak like that!"

"What are you — "

He swung her through the air.

"Let me down!" she cried. "Let me go!"

"Sorry," he said as he set her on her feet. "I guess I — "

She wasn't listening anymore. Bart and Diana were staring at her from twenty feet away. Bart's eyes glared coldly at her and his face was expressionless, but Diana was red with fury. Before Holly could go to them or even call out, they turned and hurried from the auditorium.

"I thought I'd surprise you by coming down," Zack said.

She whirled around and glared at him. "You fool! You total idiot! Didn't I tell you to leave me alone? I never want to see you again in my life!"

She ran for the door, but by the time she pushed through it, Bart and Diana were nowhere to be seen. She sank down onto the floor and the tears started to spill from her eyes. Bart would never believe her!

Chapter
11

Brian poured two glasses of soda, handed one to Karen, and looked at the partying crowd. "There must be more suits in this room than at the Supreme Court," he punned.

Karen wrinkled her nose in mock disgust. "The next time you get an urge to tell a joke like that," she said, "don't try it out on me. Save it for your show." She glanced around the room. "Oh, look. There's Lily. She looks pretty happy, doesn't she?"

"She has a right to be," Brian replied. "That monologue she did this afternoon was fantastic. Most of the time I didn't know whether I wanted to laugh or cry. It's no wonder she took first place."

Karen smiled. "Remember the part about hunting for a present for her dad in Woolworth's and not being able to decide whether to get him the rubber snake or the pencil box shaped like a fish?

She practically had me convinced she was eight years old."

"Yeah. It's amazing when you remember her background. You'd think she would be a lot more bitter. Hey, you stay right here a minute, okay? I just want to go over and set a time to get that kid on tape, before she gets too famous to bother with the likes of me."

"Sure," Karen said indulgently. "And tell her the interview we did will be in Friday's issue. I'll call the printer on Monday with a new lead about her win today."

"She's only been at Kennedy a short while," Brian said, shaking his head, "and already she's a celebrity. She sure deserves it."

He walked over and started talking to Lily. Karen scooped up some cheese dip with a corn chip and wandered around the party. She would have expected a roomful of debaters to be terribly earnest and dull, full of intense conversations about types of evidence and proper argument structure. There were one or two of those going on, but for the most part the kids in the room seemed just like anyone else. Most of them were dressed as if they had just come from a job interview at a Fortune 500 corporation, but so what? If this had been a tennis tournament, Karen figured, lots of them would have been wearing tennis whites.

"Smile!" someone commanded.

She turned curiously just as Dee clicked the shutter.

"Award-winning editor at distinguished soiree," Dee said.

"Award? What award?"

"Give it time. You'll win one someday." She paused as her eyes searched the room for a potentially good shot, as she always did when she had her camera with her. Not seeing any snappable scenes just then, she turned back to Karen. "How about Greg and Holly winning third place — neat, isn't it? I got some nice shots of them during the debate."

"Good. Did you get any of Lily Rorshack?"

"From Stevenson? The tall thin girl with pale skin and huge eyes? No, why?"

"She's our big story here, that's why," Karen said. "It's nice that Holly and Greg took third, but Lily took a first in the humorous improvisation competition."

"Yeah?" Dee replied. "I'd be impressed if I knew what that was."

"You *would* be impressed if you'd watched her this afternoon, and even more impressed if you knew the kind of life she'd been living before she went to Stevenson. I'm putting an interview I did with her on page one next week."

"Really? I'd like to meet her." She looked around again. "Maybe I can get a shot of her tonight, before I have to split."

"Try," Karen urged. "It would be great to have a photo of her to run with the article."

Dee went off to meet Lily. Karen resumed her stroll around the room, stopping to talk to some Kennedy kids who had come down for the tournament. Finally she saw Greg, who was leaning against the wall, hands in the pockets of his navy blue wool suit, listening to a guy in a plaid sport jacket who was talking very fast. Greg caught Karen's eye and excused himself.

"Wow," he said as they walked away together, "I just had to listen to blow-by-blow accounts of his three most recent debates. What gets me is that he was so sure I'd be fascinated by them."

"And were you?"

"Absolutely." Greg closed his eyes, tipped his head to one side, and made a snoring noise.

Karen laughed, then said, "By the way, congratulations. You must really be pleased to have done so well in the tournament."

"Thanks. The one who really deserves the credit is Holly. She did a super job of researching the topic and putting together our case, and her speeches really impressed the judge."

"Okay, I'll congratulate her, then, too. I haven't seen her this evening. Is she around?"

"I'm not sure. Something got her pretty upset earlier. She told me she didn't know if she could handle a party, or if she even felt like trying."

"That's too bad," said Karen. Her gaze strayed around the room. Lily was over near the windows now, delivering another monologue to a growing circle of listeners. Brian was standing next to her, listening intently. Suddenly her audience laughed loudly. The rest of the room got very quiet for a moment or two as people turned to see what was going on, and then the normal buzz of conversation resumed.

"Lily's always on," Greg said with a shrug. "Listen, Karen, I still don't understand about K.C. Didn't she explain why she wasn't coming?"

"I told you, all she said was that she had too

122

much homework. I didn't really understand it, either. Does she have an exam coming up soon or something?"

He frowned. "I don't think so. That's funny, because she didn't say anything about homework when I talked to her this morning. She said she felt tired after seeing the doctor and having the cast changed."

"She did look tired," Karen said. "I guess it hasn't been easy for her since the accident."

"It hasn't been easy for me, either."

Karen glanced significantly at his leg. "Oh? I don't notice any cast or crutches," she said.

Greg flushed. "Okay, okay! I know she's had a hard time of it. But we've been planning this for *weeks*! How could she just flake out on me like that? At least she could have made an effort!"

Karen fiddled with the empty cup in her hands, wishing that Emily were there. She would know exactly what to say to Greg in the mood he was in. The reason her Candy Hearts column was so popular was that she could be sensible and sensitive, involved and detached, all at the same time. Not Karen. She was flipping back and forth between being furious at Katie for letting Greg down so badly, and being furious at Greg for being so self-centered and insensitive. She was trying hard not to let either reaction show. She tried to think of some way to change the subject. Just then she looked toward the door, and let out a small sigh of relief.

"Oh, look," she said, "Jonathan's here. I didn't know he was coming down."

"No? He gave Dee a lift. Didn't you see him at the debate?"

Karen's cheeks grew warm. She had hoped Greg and Holly wouldn't find out that she hadn't been to the debating finals. "Er, no," she said. "I, uh, figured I ought to cover the humorous improv finals instead. I just interviewed Lily for the paper, so. . . ." She trailed off into an embarrassed silence.

"Got it," he said easily. "Don't worry, you didn't miss much. Oil import taxes are pretty dry stuff compared to humorous monologues — especially Lily's. Speaking of dry, I need another soda. How about you?"

"No, thanks. But you go ahead. I'm going to do some more mingling."

Across the room, practically hidden by a large potted plant, Holly sat alone at a table and studied the backs of her hands. In her mind she saw once again, for the hundredth time, the look on Bart's face when Zachary rushed up and hugged her in front of everyone. By the time she managed to disentangle herself, he and Diana had already disappeared.

Why hadn't Bart given her a chance to explain? If the situation had been reversed, she would have given him a chance — even a dozen chances, and then a dozen more if he needed them. After their time together that morning, how could he think for even one moment that she loved anyone but him?

Still, she couldn't really blame him. She remembered that she had sometimes wondered whether he was becoming interested in any of the girls he'd met at college. So it would have been only natural, especially considering how jealous Bart could be, for him to wonder whether she was attracted to someone else. It happened all the time. And then for him to have to sit there and see the girl he loved in another guy's arms, in front of all those people! Everyone in the auditorium must have thought she and Zack were a couple. Bart must have felt humiliated and betrayed.

And Diana . . . was it only a week since she had confronted Diana and forced her to listen? Holly had promised that there was nothing at all between her and Zack, that she was totally faithful to Bart. Diana had believed her, only to see something that made her think Holly had lied. Of course, Diana must have been deeply hurt to find out that her best friend had deceived her.

Holly pressed her lips together to stop them from trembling. In Diana's place, she thought, she would have acted differently. Holly would have tried to understand what had happened. She would have wondered how she could have been so wrong about someone she thought she knew so well. And Holly would have questioned whether she might be mistaken about what she *thought* she saw.

But Diana was more impetuous than Holly was. And after all, she *had* seen Holly and Zack together at the Valentine's Day Dance. Why should she question evidence her own eyes had provided?

"Hi, Holly. Congratulations."

She looked up and refocused her gaze. "Oh. Hi, Jonathan. Thanks."

He pushed his Indiana Jones hat back from his face and looked at her for a long moment. Then he pulled out the chair across from her and sat down. "Am I mistaken, or are you the girl who just finished third in a very high-powered forensics tournament?" he asked.

"That's right," she said, puzzled.

"Ah. Did you come down here expecting to do a lot better than third place?"

"Not at all. I was hoping we'd make the finals, but I didn't think we'd be in the top four."

"Uh-huh. Then why are you sitting here in the corner all by yourself, looking like someone just died?"

"Why, I . . . I. . . ." To her horror, tears began to trickle down her cheeks.

"Hey, I'm sorry," Jonathan said. "I didn't mean to upset you."

"Oh, it's not your fault," she said with a sniff. "I was already upset."

From the other side of the room, a Bon Jovi tape came on, very loud. Holly winced.

Jonathan leaned closer so she could hear him. "Am I right that you're not in the mood for a party just now?"

She nodded dismally. All she really wanted to do was go home and go to bed. But home was a hundred miles away.

Jonathan must have been reading her mind. "I'm driving back to Rose Hill tonight," he said. "Would you like a ride?"

"Would I! When?"

He glanced around. "Well, I'm supposed to give Dee a ride home, so let me go find out how much longer she wants to hang out."

"Great. I'll go tell Ms. Woodbury that I'm going home tonight, then find a phone and tell my mom. Thanks, Jonathan."

She leaned across the table and kissed his cheek. He grinned and patted her head. As he walked away, she found herself thinking how lucky she was that Bart and Diana hadn't been there watching — they might have misinterpreted *that*, too.

The entire center of the room was taken up by dancing couples. They all looked like they were having a fantastic time. And why not? They had survived the intense pressure of the tournament, and now was their chance to cut loose a little.

Greg sprawled on a sofa and watched. All his friends were gone: Karen and Brian had left earlier, and now Jonathan and Dee and even Holly had decided to head home. He really felt like celebrating his victory — in a tournament like this, against teams like these, third place really was a victory — but he had no one to celebrate with, and he didn't feel like partying alone.

It was mostly Katie's fault, he thought moodily. If she had come to Charlottesville as she had promised, they would both be having a wonderful evening. They might not be spinning wildly on the dance floor — that was asking a little too much of a girl with her leg in a cast — but they would be laughing and kidding and letting the good times roll. Instead, the good times were rolling right past him.

"Hi, Greg. Can I sit down?"

Roxanne was standing there, looking spectacular. He sat up. Greg had barely escaped her stunt at the Valentine's Day Dance, and he knew she was about as safe and trustworthy as a rattlesnake, but that didn't seem to matter at that particular moment. "Sure," he said, "sit."

"You know," she confided, "I've been waiting all evening for a chance to tell you how thrilled I was to watch you in the tournament today. You were awesome!"

"Oh, well," he began, "I wouldn't — "

"I am telling you the one hundred percent truth," she insisted. "You deserved first place instead of third, and if you had had a teammate who was as sharp and intelligent as you are, you would have gotten it, too. I can't tell you how exciting the whole thing was for me. It was like watching an intellectual Grand Prix race, and you were the fastest, smoothest driver around."

One part of Greg knew he shouldn't listen to any more of such blatant flattery, but another part of him didn't want it to stop. At that moment someone switched off the heavy metal. A second later the sounds of a slow, romantic tune filled the air.

"Hey," he said, "do you want to dance?"

Roxanne looked deep into his eyes. "I'd love to," she said.

The moment they were standing, she was in his arms.

* * *

Holly waved to Dee and Jonathan, then went up the walk. The moment she opened the front door, her mother hurried over to give her a hug. She was carrying a fat envelope in her left hand.

"This came today," she explained, giving it to Holly. "I wanted to tell you when you called, but I thought you'd want to open it yourself."

The return address showed that it was from the director of admissions at the University of Montana. Holly looked at the envelope with a sudden feeling of dread. What did the letter inside say? She would know that in a moment. But what did she *want* the letter to say? She no longer knew that, after what had happened tonight. One way or another, though, her life was changing, and it was up to her to make the right choices.

"Aren't you going to open it?" her mother asked.

"Hmm? Oh . . . sure." She ripped the flap and pulled out the contents. Forms, booklets, forms. . . . There was the letter at last.

Dear Ms. Daniels:
- We are pleased to inform you that your application. . . .

"I'm in," she said quickly, knowing her mother was about ready to die from curiosity. Then she skimmed the letter, looking for the all-important paragraph about financial aid. She found it, read it, and did the numbers in her head. "They're giving me enough money, too," she added.

"Sweetheart, how wonderful!" her mother exclaimed, giving her another hug. "It's exactly what you've been hoping for and working toward all year. And if anybody deserves it, you do!"

Holly tried to share her mother's joy, but she couldn't. She kept remembering Bart's face as he stormed out of the auditorium that afternoon. What if it was all over between them? How could she stand being at a college where the only person she knew — the guy she was in love with — refused to speak to her?

Maybe the news would change his attitude, or at least make him listen long enough for her to explain. She dragged herself to the telephone and dialed the Einersons' number.

Diana answered. The moment she heard Holly's voice, her own became icy.

"Can I speak to Bart?" Holly said. "I've got some news for him."

"I've got some news for *you*," Diana retorted. "My brother went to bed early, because he's changed his plans. He's going back to Montana on the first flight tomorrow."

"He is? But — " Holly closed her eyes and tried to think. How could she ever explain if she couldn't talk to him? "Will you give him a message before he goes?" she said. "It's very important."

"I certainly won't," Diana replied.

"Di — "

"He told me tonight that he never wants to hear your name again. And he won't hear it from me."

"But Di — "

Diana had already hung up. Holly took the

receiver away from her ear and stared at it in disbelief. After a couple of seconds she woodenly put it back in its cradle. With a heart heavy as lead, she trudged up the stairs to her room, a single tear running down her cheek.

Chapter
12

Jonathan tossed his hat on the grass, leaned back on his arms, and raised his face to the sun. "Ah, that feels good," he said. "First rays of the season. I bet the maple trees like it, too. Right, Diana?"

Diana took the question seriously. "Yes and no," she replied. "What you need for a really good sugaring season is a string of warm days and cold nights. It's really interesting how the weather affects the production of maple syrup. Come to the festival on Saturday and you can learn all about it."

Karen smiled to herself. Diana was doing her best to generate enthusiasm for the upcoming Maple Sugarin' Festival, but for now the crowd was far more interested in simply eating lunch outdoors for the first time since the fall. As a sign that spring was approaching, the migration outdoors for lunch didn't quite rank with daffodils or the first robin, but it was pretty reliable all the same.

She nibbled a carrot stick and looked around at her friends. Eric and Colin were arguing about the answer to a question on the most recent history test. Pamela was doing a sketch of Molly, who was telling Elise what it was like to go to high school in southern California. Except for the climate, it didn't sound all that different from Kennedy. Jonathan and Matt were talking about something in low voices. Cars, probably. Jeremy was explaining to Emily and Dee that back in England this weather would be considered unseasonably warm compared to the usual chill. Dee, wrapping her scarf tighter, looked unconvinced by his comment.

Karen sighed. They were a good bunch. It was sad to think that in a few short months each of them would be going off in a different direction and that they would never really be together as a group again.

Dee sat down next to her and took a celery stalk. "Are you covering the Maple Sugarin' Festival yourself?" she asked.

"You bet," Karen said with a smile. "It was either that or sign up for one of Diana's committees of volunteers. I decided I would rather take notes than pick up litter."

"Good thinking. I ended up promising to let the Wilderness Club have a look at the photos I take. That's okay with you, isn't it?"

"I don't think it will create any problems," Karen replied after a moment's thought. "As long as you remember that you're mainly taking pictures for the paper. They'll probably only want a few, anyway." Karen snapped her fingers. "Speaking of pictures, I decided what to use for the forensics tournament piece. The ones you took of Lily at the party were very cute, but none of them worked in context. All you saw was her talking and a group of kids listening. So I went with the one of Greg at the podium, gesturing at the ceiling, and that nice one of him and Holly hugging each other when the judge announced they'd won."

"Good choices," Dee said. "Hey, do you have any idea what's with Holly? At the debate she was really flying, but that night when she came back with us, you would have thought she'd wound up in last place instead of third."

Karen lowered her voice. "My guess is boy trouble," she said.

"You mean — " Dee glanced significantly in the direction of Diana.

"Uh-huh. Boy trouble *and* best friend trouble. I saw her with the two of them at lunch in Charlottesville, talking and laughing, and everything looked fine. But I didn't notice them after the debate, did you?"

"Now that you mention it . . . no." Dee frowned. "Of course, they might have had to get back for some family stuff or something."

"Sure. And if you believe that, how about a date with Tom Cruise tonight?"

"Shows what you know. I had a date with him *last* night." Dee smiled for a moment, then turned serious. "Maybe something did happen with Bart and Diana. Whatever it was, she sure was upset.

After English class this morning she could hardly drag herself out of her seat. And you know what a bundle of energy she usually is."

"I can't be a guide," Elise protested. "I don't know a sugar maple from a banana tree!"

"We'll teach you," Diana insisted. "We're having a training session on Friday after school. Besides, you don't have to be an expert. All you're supposed to do is tell people where to find the different events and exhibits, and we'll give you a schedule and a map in case you need to look anything up."

"Why not just give the schedule and map to people when they come in?"

"We will, but you'd be surprised how many people have trouble reading a schedule, and find maps totally baffling. What do you say, Elise?"

"Say yes," Jeremy advised.

"Volunteers get a special edition festival T-shirt," Diana added.

"There's a picture of a sap bucket on it," Jeremy pointed out. "It's simply dashing. Once people see you in it, everyone will want one."

"Oh, all right," Elise said, "but I still don't think — "

"Great." Diana wrote Elise's name in her notebook. "I'll remind you later in the week about our meeting on Friday."

She looked around. Most of the people she had asked to help had agreed, whether from an interest in the festival, school spirit, or a lack of anything better to do on Saturday. Was there anyone in the crowd she hadn't approached yet?

There *was* one person, of course. She hadn't asked Holly, and she wasn't going to. She didn't trust herself to speak to her, even about something as impersonal as the festival. It wasn't that she was still very angry at Holly; she had gotten over that pretty quickly. What had happened had happened. Nothing could be done about it now, and there was no reason to stay angry. But she was terribly disappointed in Holly — and sad, too, because she could never think of Holly as a friend again. A friend was someone you knew you could trust, someone who would never lie to you, someone you knew would never hurt you. But after acting that way with Zack, it was clear that Holly had lied to her. And Bart had been completely devastated! How could anyone do what Holly had done to her best friend, and the boy she loved?

It would have been different if Holly and Bart had broken up, Diana thought. She would have found that difficult to handle, because she would have wanted to be loyal to both her brother and her friend. But she would have understood, and she would have been able to sympathize with both of them. Everyone knew how hard it was when one of the members of a couple went away to school, and everyone knew that lots of couples didn't last when that happened. Look at Chris Austin and Greg Montgomery. They had been as much in love as anybody, but after Chris went off to college, they couldn't keep the old feelings going. No one blamed either of them for that.

No, what bothered her about Holly was her dishonesty. She kept claiming that she was still deeply in love with Bart, but when she thought no one was looking, she sneaked off with someone else. Holly had lied to her, saying that she wasn't going to have any more to do with Zack, in order to persuade her to keep the truth from Bart. And Diana had agreed not to tell him anything about what had happened because she had believed Holly.

But when Bart came up to her at the debate and asked her straight out if there was anything going on between this Zack and Holly, what could she do? Lie to her own brother? It looked as if Roxanne had told Bart about Holly and Zack. If Roxanne knew about it, probably a lot of other kids did, too. Maybe that Zack kid from Stevenson had even been going around bragging to all his friends about how he was cutting in on a former Kennedy football star's girl. The guys would love that.

"Di, are you feeling all right?"

"What?" She looked up. Jeremy was watching her with a look of concern on his face.

"It's nearly time for class. Didn't you hear me before?"

"Sorry," she said. "I was thinking about something."

"Some*thing*?" he said, giving her a shrewd glance. "Or some*one*?"

Diana sighed. She had told Jeremy all about what had happened. She rested her head against his shoulder. She knew she should just forget about the whole mess and get on with her life, but she felt so miserable.

* * *

Katie stirred her chocolate pudding and studied the pattern of the swirls left by the spoon as if it might reveal the future. But she wasn't at all sure that she really wanted to know what the future held. Coping with the present was difficult enough.

She pushed the pudding away from her in disgust. She had to remember that she couldn't eat whatever she liked anymore. Her body was used to a lot more activity than she'd been getting since she broke her leg, and she was beginning to get flabby. Great — all she needed was to gain weight. Just one more thing to feel bad about.

The rest of the lunch table was empty. Holly had been there earlier, but she had been as silent and moody as Katie. The moment she'd finished her sandwich and milk, she left. Everyone else was probably still out in the quad. Katie had seen them there on her way to the lunchroom, but she didn't feel up to being social. Just getting from one place to another took most of her energy.

She felt a hand on her shoulder and heard Greg say, "I was looking all over for you. What are you doing in here by yourself?"

"Eating lunch." As she said the words, she realized that they had a nasty edge to them that she hadn't intended. She tried to make up for it by adding, "I didn't want to hang around outside. My toes get cold."

He pulled out the chair next to her and sat down. "What about those big wool socks I gave you? Did you try one on? Did it fit over the cast?"

"I tried it, but . . . gray socks with bright red

toes and heels? I feel conspicuous enough already without looking like a clown."

"Oh. I'll take them back, then. They're my favorite crew socks." He paused. "I was just trying to help you be a little more comfortable, you know."

She gave the pudding another stir. There didn't seem to be anything to say.

Greg cleared his throat. "I just saw Diana," he said. "She was telling me all about the Maple Sugarin' Festival on Saturday. It sounds like a lot of fun. They're expecting a huge crowd."

"Are they?" she said listlessly. "That's nice."

"What do you say? You want to go?"

She gave her head a little shake. "I don't know, Greg, I — "

"Come on. You could use some fresh air and exercise. And we can take along a folding chair, in case you get tired of standing."

She imagined herself outside, surrounded by cheerful, active people, and shuddered. "I don't think I'm up to it," she said.

"Sure you are. We don't have to make a big deal out of it."

"Anyway, I have an appointment on Saturday with the physical therapist."

He leaned forward. "Okay, here's what we'll do. I'll take you to your appointment, hang out till you're done, and we'll go to the festival. How's that?"

Why did he keep insisting? Couldn't he see that she just wanted to be left alone? "I can't," she said. "Really."

He looked annoyed. "So what are you going to

do instead?" he demanded. "Sit at home and mope, the way you did last weekend?"

"Why do you sound so mad?"

"Because I *am* mad, that's why! You promised to come down to Charlottesville, and you didn't show up. I was looking forward to having you there, and you disappointed me. And now it sounds like you're going to do it to me again."

She felt herself tense. "I'm not doing anything to you," she said coolly. "I'm staying away from something I don't want to go to, that's all. It doesn't have anything to do with you."

"Of course it does! We — "

She broke in. "Anyway, from what I heard about what went on at Charlottesville, you didn't stay disappointed for long! Didn't you have Roxanne Easton there to help you get over it?"

"Oh, for — ! Okay! I danced with Roxanne a couple of times. So what? Are you going to make a federal case out of it?"

She told herself she should lay off. She knew Roxanne didn't mean a thing to Greg . . . and Katie also knew that she meant a whole lot to him.

But it was hard for her to really *believe* that she still meant a lot to him. Before Katie had broken her leg she had known who she was — Katie Crawford, gymnast. Gymnastics had been something she was really good at, something she could center her life around. With a broken leg she was no longer a gymnast, though, and that had changed the whole way she saw herself. When she looked in the mirror in the morning all she saw was a girl who couldn't do *anything* without help anymore. She felt like she couldn't have fun anymore, and she couldn't see how anyone else could have fun when she was around, either.

That was it. She was terrified that Greg would stop wanting to be with her, now that she wasn't as much fun to be with. And that made her push him. Even though he had been so patient and cheerful with her for so long, she kept trying to make him *admit* that he didn't want to be with her. He had passed so many tests already, but that didn't count. She still woke up in the middle of the night shaking with fear that he might not pass the next one.

She looked at him with tortured eyes. She couldn't stop herself from saying it. "It was more than a couple of times, from what I heard."

"If it was, you've got no one but yourself to blame," he said hotly. "If you hadn't copped out on me, I wouldn't have even *looked* at Roxanne. But there I was, trying to unwind after a very tense two days, and you were back at home sitting around feeling sorry for yourself. I felt like dancing, Roxanne felt like dancing, so we danced. Big deal. And you certainly know how Roxanne exaggerates her little stories."

"I'm sure you didn't find the experience too painful," Katie said with a sneer.

He shot up out of his chair and towered over her. "You're right," Greg said. "I didn't. In fact, I even enjoyed it. You'd be surprised what a treat it was to be around someone who wasn't a total downer. Someone who still remembers how to have fun now and then."

She struggled up to a standing position, holding onto the table for support. "Someone who didn't break her leg, you mean!"

The agony she was feeling must have shown on her face. Greg reached over to take her arm. In a softer voice, he said, "Look K.C., I know what a hard time you've been having. I've watched you struggle every day. I want to help you in any way I can. But you've got to be willing to let me help, and you've got to be willing to help yourself."

She felt tears well up in her eyes, but instead of softening her mood, they made her even more determined to make Greg feel as much pain as she herself was feeling. "Was that what you were doing with Roxanne?" she demanded. "Trying to help yourself?"

Greg's face turned even redder. He slammed his hand on the table. "Roxanne can go take a long walk on a short pier, for all I care! I'm talking about *you*. Can't you do anything besides mope and complain? Look at you, sitting in here all by yourself while your friends are out enjoying the sunshine. What's the matter, afraid they might manage to cheer you up?"

"You don't know what it's like for me!"

"That's right, I don't. But I know this. You said you were going to fight this thing, and I said I'd help. But you don't have the guts to fight it. You were fine as long as everything was going your way, but the first time you run into a problem, you turn into a quitter."

"And the first time you're at a party without me, you take off after whatever's available! It's just like when those girls came over from Sweden, you couldn't wait to start chasing one of them. Well, go ahead, chase Roxanne Easton all you like! *I* won't stand in your way!"

He stared at her for a moment, then said, "That is the only sensible thing you've said in about a week." Without another word, he turned and walked out of the lunchroom.

Katie watched him go, her cheeks wet with tears. Then she grabbed her crutch and smashed it against the table. She couldn't care less if it broke in a billion pieces.

Chapter
13

Greg paused for a moment near the food tent. A boy and girl taking a break from all the events of the Maple Sugarin' Festival were feeding each other little bits of maple sugar candy. They were sitting close together, trying to toss small pieces of candy into each other's mouths. One of them missed and they both laughed, then hugged each other tightly.

Greg turned and walked away. He couldn't bear to watch couples be so happy together. It reminded him too strongly that Katie was not there with him. He had been at the Nature Center since midmorning, trying to construct booths, set up exhibits, and carry whatever needed carrying. At one point, he even climbed up into a tree to tie one end of the banner that welcomed people to the festival. It was fun to be working hard with people he liked, but whenever the pace slacked off, he found himself missing Katie and wishing she were there.

Why had they had that stupid quarrel? Once he got angry, he ended up saying things he didn't really mean, with no easy way to take them back. He only hoped that the same thing had happened to Katie. If not, if she really meant everything she said, then their future was already a thing of the past. And that was the last thing he wanted.

Just ahead, next to a scarred old tree, one of the Nature Center staff was explaining how sap was collected. Greg strolled over to listen.

"The Indians used to tap maples by making V-shaped slashes in the tree and catching the sap in birchbark dishes," the naturalist told the small crowd. "European settlers learned how from watching the Indians. . . ."

Greg let his mind wander. The sun felt warm on his head and shoulders, but the breeze that ruffled his hair still had the bite of winter to it. The aromas it brought carried an even stronger hint of good things to eat. The pancake booth was obviously working at capacity, and hamburgers were starting to sizzle somewhere.

Jonathan came over. In his hand was an intricately twisted piece of crispy fried dough with lines of syrup across it. It looked almost like a piece of abstract sculpture — except that Jonathan was biting off the end of it. He noticed Greg looking at him curiously.

"Funnel cake," he explained. "They pour doughnut batter into the hot oil with a funnel. Want to try it?"

Greg took a piece and nibbled at it. "Not bad," he said. "It tastes better than it looks."

Jonathan held it at arm's length. "It does look

a little bizarre, doesn't it? But that's good. People are so chicken about trying anything new that the line for the funnel cake booth is a whole lot shorter than the pancake line. This is my third." He took another bite.

Greg's stomach rumbled. "I think I'll get one, too," he said. "Catch you later."

Once he was at the food booths, he found it hard to stop at one crazy-looking doughnut. He finished it off in a half dozen bites, wiped the syrup from his fingers, and decided to try some homemade shortbread flavored with maple syrup. That left him thirsty. He bought a cup of hot chocolate and started back to the exhibit area before anything else could tempt him.

When he got there, a young woman was demonstrating how to carry two full sap buckets using a shoulder yoke. He spotted Emily watching from a perch on an antique wooden sleigh. He walked over to say hi.

"Hi. How's Katie doing?" Emily asked. "Is she here today?"

Greg looked away. "No, she had a physical therapy session this morning, and she's always bushed afterward."

"Oh." After a silence, Emily said, "I feel bad for her. She's having a very rough time. But I don't have to tell you that. She was so caught up in her gymnastics, and she was such a competitor. It must seem like the end of everything to be suddenly unable to compete like that."

"I guess so," Greg replied. "But if she's such a competitor, why doesn't she make more of an effort? Where did all her spunk go? Broken legs do heal, after all."

Emily frowned thoughtfully. "Sure they do. But suppose you've always counted on something, just taken it for granted without even thinking. What if it suddenly goes wrong on you? That can really shake you up. I hate to drive my dad's car because one time it stalled on me in heavy traffic, and I couldn't get it to start again. It only happened that one time, but I don't trust it anymore. Katie's always known that her body would do most of the things she asked it to. Now, all of a sudden, it won't do even simple things. She might know in her mind that she'll recover and be back where she was before the accident, but how does she make herself *believe* it?"

"I don't know," Greg said slowly. "But I don't think I can do it for her. I'm not even sure I can help."

Karen made some notes for her article as she and Brian strolled down the row of crafts demonstrations. She was planning to explain how maple syrup was made, of course, but she wanted to try to catch the spirit of the event in her article as well. It was a celebration of the fact that spring was just around the corner — everyone could hardly wait.

One thing she certainly intended to mention in the paper was the terrific turnout by the kids from Kennedy, both those who had been there a long time, and those who had just transferred from Stevenson. People still tended to hang out with others from their own group, but most kids were also waving, nodding, and saying hello to people they recognized, whether they were old or new Cardinals. Karen hoped that some of the tension created by the arrival of the Stevenson students was starting to disappear.

"Darn," Brian said. "We missed the sheep shearing by fifteen minutes."

Karen giggled. "Gosh," she said in an exaggerated voice. "That was going to be the highlight of the festival for me!"

"Sorry to disappoint you," he retorted. "Would some pancakes with real maple syrup console you?"

"Well . . . they might. Let's go see."

As they neared the refreshment tent, they could smell the pancakes cooking. So could everyone else in the neighborhood, and it gave most of them the same idea.

"Yikes!" Karen said. "Look at that line!"

Brian surveyed it with a gloomy expression. "We could go away and come back later," he said.

"And find different people in a line just as long? We'll be starved! Unh-uh."

They found the end of the line and joined it. Karen didn't really mind the wait that much. The sun warmed her, the air invigorated her, and the bright blue sky made her sigh with contentment. And when Brian put his arm around her shoulders and held her close, the only other thing she needed to be completely happy was a plate of pancakes with maple syrup.

She slowly became aware of a familiar voice

coming from ahead of them on the line. It was Lily. She brought her mind back to full attention and listened in.

"The worst part of being an only child," Lily was saying, "is meals. Who do you talk to? The grown-ups? All they want to talk about is quarterly earnings and the price of tomatoes. If you try to tell them what happened to He-Man that afternoon, they threaten to pull the plug on the TV. And when you discover how to flip a pea with your fork, are they impressed with your new skill? Do they encourage you to try to get into the Guinness Book of World Records by flipping a pea farther and more accurately than anyone else? Not a chance! Instead, they stop serving peas in the hope that you'll eventually forget how to flip them. In the meantime, of course, you've figured out how to flip carrots, pork chops — and especially mashed potatoes."

The kids standing around Lily cracked up. One of them was Daniel. When he noticed Karen he stopped laughing, but Karen gave him a pleasant smile and a wave. She wasn't going to play into his idea of a feud if she could help it.

"That's why I always liked to eat dinner with friends who had brothers and sisters," Lily continued. "As long as you didn't make too much noise or too much mess, you could do whatever you wanted, and there was always somebody there to do it with. You could shove your lima beans onto the baby's plate and take his French fries in exchange. You could dip your hamburger in your apple juice to see what it was going to be like when it got all mixed up in your stomach.

149

You could even tickle each other's feet under the table and see who started laughing first. You had to be careful, of course. If you started tickling the wrong feet, somebody might misunderstand."

Her friends cracked up again. Karen laughed, too, but suddenly she got a strange feeling in the pit of her stomach. She poked Brian in the ribs.

"Hey, what was that for?" he demanded loudly.

"Shh! Listen to Lily."

"I am," he protested. "She has quite a range, doesn't she? At Charlottesville her character was sort of bittersweet, but this one is just plain funny."

Karen watched her for a minute and then said, "Brian, Lily isn't an only child, is she?"

"Huh? No, of course not. She has a brother who got hit in the head with a bottle, remember?"

"Sure I do, but suppose you didn't know that. I'd never know she was an only child. Lily turns her characters on and off like they were light switches."

"She's very convincing," Brian replied.

"As convincing as she was the day Daniel brought her to meet us?" Karen asked.

"Maybe even more so. This character is one anybody can relate to, but her own story is so amazing that it's hard to believe."

Karen shook her head. "It's unreal that someone who's been through so much can just shake off all those bad memories."

"Well, maybe she becomes these various characters to forget about the unhappiness . . . you know, it's like an escape method," Brian said.

"Right," Karen answered. "Fortunately for Lily, her humor saved her. Other people might not have been strong enough to pull themselves out of trouble." She paused for a minute before saying, "It's possible our article may help lots of other kids."

"Let's hope so," Brian responded. "Lily's really special. . . . "

"Mmmm." Karen laughed at another one of Lily's sharp lines, then repeated, "Unreal. She's almost too good to be true."

Chapter
14

"Here, young lady, taste this."

Holly obediently took the small chunk of solidified maple sugar offered to her by a man dressed as a nineteenth century sugar maker. It was very sweet, but unlike regular sugar it had another taste in addition to its sweetness. It reminded her of a time when she was little, eating waffles and reading the funnies on Sunday morning. Would she ever again be able to enjoy such simple pleasures? She hoped so, but right now the future looked very bleak.

The only reason she had dragged herself to the Maple Sugarin' Festival was that her mom had pretty much ordered her to go, telling her that she was tired of seeing her dragging around the house. Holly had to admit that she was grateful to have something to distract her from her thoughts of Bart.

As she turned to go back up the hill, she noticed Pamela sitting on a nearby bench, an open sketchbook on her lap. Pamela looked up and waved. As Holly came closer she saw that Pamela was working on a pencil sketch of the sugar house.

"I like that," Holly said. "It's got a very rugged feeling to it."

Pamela held the book at arm's length and studied the sketch dispassionately. "It's not bad," she finally said. "The proportions aren't quite right, though. How are you doing?"

The question took Holly by surprise. Did everyone know about what had happened? "All right, I guess," she replied. "Well, not so hot, to tell you the truth."

"That's what I figured. Here, look." She flipped back through the sketchbook and stopped at a page. "I did this the day we came back to school after our snow days."

There was Holly, exuberant and laughing, with a snowball in her hand. "Pam," Holly exclaimed, "that's terrific! Hey, is there any way I can make a copy of it? My mom would be so thrilled if I could give her something like that."

"You can have this one," Pamela said. "I'll put fixative on it when I get home this afternoon so it won't smudge. But this is the other thing I wanted you to see. I did this in study hall on Thursday."

The charcoal drawing showed Holly slumped in her chair. She was holding a book open in front of her, but she wasn't looking at it. Her gaze was aimed into the distance, as if she were contemplating a bleak landscape. Weariness and despair showed in her posture and on her face.

"I don't know what's happened to you in the last week . . ." Pamela began.

"It's a long story," Holly muttered.

"Whatever it is, it can't be worth feeling this way about." She gestured toward the sketch. "Did you know that Matt and I broke up?"

Holly nodded. "Jonathan told me the other day. I'm sorry."

"So am I. So's Matt. We both feel horrible about it. But we're trying to keep our minds on what's going to matter to us in the long run, not just in the next few days or weeks or months. It's never easy to figure out what's really important, but you have to try."

"I see what you mean," said Holly. "Have you ever thought of taking over Emily's column in the paper?"

Pamela blushed. "I know I was butting in," she said, "but you looked so miserable that I just couldn't help dispensing some advice."

"Maybe I didn't write you a 'Dear Pamela' letter, but it's still good advice. Thanks."

"That's okay. And I won't forget about the sketch for your mom."

What was really important to her? Holly walked slowly up the hill, trying to figure out the answer. She had been in love with Bart for over a year. He was a central part of her whole life. And she and Diana had been best friends for just as long. They had shared their most private thoughts, feelings, and desires. They'd consoled each other in bad times and cheered for each other's victories. Were Bart and Diana important to her? Of course they were.

But what about going into medicine? How important was that? She had been dreaming about it, and working hard for it, ever since she could remember. She knew that dreams and goals often change, because the people who hold them change. But this dream of hers hadn't changed. If anything, it had become stronger, and more real with each step she took toward making it come true. And whether she went to college with Bart, as she had hoped and planned, or without him, she was going to —

"Hello, Holly. I said hello before, but I guess you didn't hear me."

"Hello, Zack," she said, as coldly as she could. "What do you want?"

"Want? I . . . I . . . nothing, I guess. I just wanted to say hello."

"Why? To get me in more trouble than I'm already in? Is it revenge you want? I told you I didn't want to talk to you again. Why didn't you listen to what I said?"

He turned bright red. "Hey, listen," Zachary said. "I'm sorry, okay? I don't know why you act like saying hello is an insult, but whatever I did, I'm sorry I did it. Is that good enough?"

Holly imagined Diana coming up the path and catching her deep in conversation with Zachary. "No, it isn't," she said. "Just go away. *Please!*"

She saw the pain in his eyes, and part of her wanted to apologize or at least to try to explain. After all, he wasn't responsible for the horrible situation she was in. But why couldn't he take a hint?

"It was just a game with you the whole time,

wasn't it?" Zachary said angrily. "Get the poor sucker to fall in love with you, then toss him overboard when you don't need him anymore. Well, you socked it to me good. I just hope that someday somebody does the same thing to you, so you know how it feels. And when you do, you can look in the mirror and ask yourself, 'How could I hurt somebody like that?'"

"Say whatever you like," she replied, becoming angry in turn. "Just say it someplace else."

"Don't worry, I'm going. I wouldn't want my presence to pollute your air."

He spun on his heel abruptly and walked quickly away. Holly almost wanted to call him back and talk things out, but she was afraid he might misinterpret anything she said as being some kind of encouragement. Anyway, she was sorry that he felt so bad, but hadn't he brought it on himself? Even after she had told him it was all over, he had come down to Charlottesville, made a public spectacle of himself and her, and probably ruined her life. *His* feelings were hurt? Too bad! Hers were hurt a whole lot worse and maybe it was all his fault after all.

"Who cares about maple syrup?" Roxanne demanded.

Frankie blinked. "Actually I think it's very interesting," she said. "I liked seeing how they boil down the sap and all."

"*Bo*-ring," said Roxanne. "Next thing you know they'll put on a Honey Festival and expect us to stand around watching a lot of bees buzz."

Frankie thought she knew why Rox was feeling so cross. There were too many people at the Maple Sugarin' Festival for her to stand out, and Roxanne hated to be simply part of a crowd.

They were looking at an exhibit of handmade quilts. Or at least Frankie was. Roxanne's eyes kept scanning the people who walked by.

"Who are you looking for?" Frankie asked.

"Anybody," Roxanne replied. "Anybody who matters."

Frankie had known Rox too long to be insulted by that comment. In Roxanne's terms, the only people who mattered were guys. And not just any guys, either, just guys who were good-looking and important. But of course, a girl as pretty and bright as Rox couldn't be bothered with just anybody.

A couple of booths down was a demonstration area. Frankie noticed that Greg Montgomery was standing there, talking to a man whose rolled-up shirt sleeves revealed amazing muscles. The leather apron he wore was scarred and showed burn marks. When he gestured toward a battered anvil, she realized that he must be a blacksmith.

"Let's go look at some of the other exhibits," Frankie said. "I need a new belt, and there was a booth selling them over that way."

"Not now," Roxanne said. She glanced past Frankie in the direction of Greg and the blacksmith, then went back to scanning the crowd.

Frankie thought of telling Rox that she would go look at the belts and come back, but she knew

Rox wouldn't like it. It would seem too much like Frankie was deserting her, and Rox definitely did not like being deserted.

She was moving to the other side of the booth to take a closer look at an especially colorful quilt when she saw Zachary coming up the hill. Her heart gave a little leap. He hadn't seen her yet, and she watched him as he came toward the booth where she was standing. He looked unhappy and angry. As he walked past Greg and the blacksmith, Greg waved to him and Zack only nodded stiffly in reply.

Then he glanced over and saw Roxanne and Frankie. He changed direction and headed toward them. Frankie caught her breath. He was deliberately coming over. Maybe there was hope for her. She didn't dare believe it yet, but she could still dream.

"Hi," Frankie said as he came up to them. She gave him a sweet, shy smile. Zack smiled back warmly.

"Hello, McGraw," Roxanne said pointedly. "Are you interested in quilts? I didn't think you were the type."

He ignored Roxanne's comment and spoke to Frankie. "I came over because I saw you here."

"That's very flattering, isn't it, Frankie?" As she said that, Roxanne was looking over Frankie's shoulder. Frankie looked back, too. Greg and the blacksmith were still talking.

"It's nice to know," Rox added, "that Stevenson High's star quarterback is still loyal to his old school, in spite of everything. You are, aren't you?"

158

He frowned. "What's there to be loyal to?" he demanded. "A junky old pile of bricks they're going to tear down this summer? They should have torn it down years ago."

"Never mind. I'll explain it to you some other time." Without another word she slipped past them and started down the path past the demonstration area. Frankie saw that the blacksmith had finished talking to Greg and had picked up his hammer and tongs again. Rox hurried past him and disappeared down the same path Greg had taken.

"I'm glad she left," Zack said.

"Are you?" asked Frankie. "Why?" She held her breath while she waited for his answer.

"I need to talk to you," he replied. "It's about Holly."

Frankie turned her head to watch a passing bird. She didn't want Zack to see how disappointed she was.

"I don't get it," he burst out. "It's not like I've been putting the moves on her or anything. I've been so careful! This past week I haven't even hinted at how crazy I am about her, because I know it makes her uncomfortable. I even tried to learn something about the things she's interested in, like debating, so I could talk to her about them. But she won't talk to me at all, about *anything*. I've heard about a dozen words from her in the past week, and they were all blatantly 'Go away!'"

Frankie thought hard. She certainly didn't want to give Zack any false hopes about Holly, but she had to be careful not to put Holly down, either. "You know, Zack," she began, "you can have two people who are really nice and who each have lots of other friends, but for some reason the two of them never get to be friends. Maybe something doesn't click between them. Or maybe it clicks for one of them but not the other. Do you know what I mean?"

"I guess so." He tugged up a weed from a nearby clump and started to tear it into tiny pieces. "But she *did* like me," he suddenly said. "I know she did. I couldn't be wrong about something like that."

"Then something must have come up, and she couldn't let herself like you anymore. I'm sorry, Zack, but if she keeps telling you to go away, that's what you'd better do. Forget her."

"I can't," he said.

"You haven't tried yet. Pull yourself together, start seeing some other girls, and maybe in time you and Holly can become friends. It's just that now may not be the best time for that."

"I don't want to start seeing other girls," he said sullenly. "I don't even *know* any other girls." Frankie's heart fell. Wasn't she standing right in front of him? "And even if I did, I'd probably end up blowing it with them the same way I blew it with Holly. What's the use?"

He touched her on the shoulder. "Thanks anyway, Franko," he said. "You're a real pal."

She watched him walk away and wondered what was wrong with her, why Zack never seemed to notice that she was a girl. Maybe it was simply the sort of situation she had been describing to him, where the chemistry was right for one person and not for the other. She was just good, old Franko — someone to come to for advice. Right now she felt like she needed some advice herself. Frankie went off to find Rox. She seemed to know all there was to know about guys. Maybe she could tell Frankie what she had to do to get Zack's attention.

Roxanne was standing in front of a big poster that described all the activities of the Rose Hill Nature Center. As Frankie came up to her from one direction, Greg Montgomery was walking past from the other. Roxanne didn't notice Frankie. She looked surprised, as if she were seeing Greg for the first time, and said, "Oh, hello, Greg. Isn't it a great day?"

Greg nodded but didn't return Roxanne's smile.

"I haven't had time to see more than a few of the exhibits yet," Roxanne continued. "How about you?"

Greg shrugged. "I've been to most of them, I guess. I'm going down to the sugar house now."

"Really? That sounds fascinating. Maybe I'll go, too."

Frankie felt desperate. She grabbed Rox's arm and said in an undertone, "Rox, I need to talk to you."

"Not now," Roxanne said through her teeth.

"But it's important. *Please!*"

Greg gave them a casual wave and strolled off.

Rox turned on Frankie. "*Well?*" she demanded. "Couldn't you see I was talking to Greg Montgomery? What's so important that it couldn't wait a few minutes?"

"It's Zachary. He doesn't think of me as anything but his pal. He even said so. What am I going to do?"

"Do?" said Roxanne. "You're not going to do anything. Just forget it, that's all. If you want to be his buddy, go ahead, but you're not going to get him to fall in love with you. No way! Face it, sweetie, you're not the kind of girl guys fall for. Especially not dumb hunks like Zachary."

"Rox! What do you mean, I'm not the kind of — " Frankie stopped short. She felt sick. "Zachary's not dumb," she finally mumbled.

"Whatever," Roxanne said with a dismissive wave of the hand. "I have to go. I have a date at the sugar house."

"But — "

"Save it," Roxanne said over her shoulder as she walked quickly down the path that Greg had taken.

Frankie stared after her for a long time, while her verdict sank in. *You're not the kind of girl guys fall for.* . . . Roxanne knew all about what guys liked. She had been born knowing most of it, and she'd been studying the subject since she was ten years old. If she said Frankie was a hopeless case, then it must be true.

She didn't know whether to sob or scream or just curl up in a very tight ball. One thing was for sure — she couldn't stay here, where so many people might see her. Frantically she looked around, then headed for the woods.

* * *

"Well, old girl," said Jeremy, "how does it feel to be responsible for a smash hit?" He slung the small camcorder over his shoulder.

Diana gave him a tired smile. "I'm glad it's going so well, but it's the people at the Nature Center who are really responsible. We just supplied them with a lot of volunteers and enthusiasm. And it's given us a great chance to let everybody at Kennedy know about the Nature Center and the Wilderness Club."

Elise wandered by and called out, "Hey, Diana, what do I do now?"

"Take it easy and enjoy yourself," Diana replied. "We'll start working on litter in half an hour or so, when the crowd starts to thin out."

"That's good advice for you, too," Jeremy observed. "You've been working nonstop since early morning. I've filmed enough of today's events to make a nice little promo video for the Nature Center, so why don't we go sit on the grass and watch those lovely cumulus clouds drift by?"

"Well. . . . It sounds like fun, but to tell you the truth, I'm sort of frazzled and I think I'd rather go for a little walk by myself. I'll be right back."

Some of the crafts exhibits were already being taken down. Diana exchanged a smile with the woman who had been demonstrating weaving, but as soon as she was past, her face grew somber again. No matter what she had told Jeremy, she hadn't really enjoyed the festival.

How could she? Every time Diana turned around, it seemed, she saw Holly wandering past, looking like she hadn't a friend in the world.

Diana hated to see her best friend so lonely and sad, and she hated even more the knowledge that she was responsible. But she hadn't had any choice, she told herself. Holly had betrayed Bart, and Diana had to take her brother's side.

She stopped and listened intently. Somebody was crying nearby. She followed the sound into the woods and saw a girl huddled on the ground, sobbing. For one awful moment she thought that it might be Holly. Then she saw it was the girl from Stevenson who had worked on the computer program for the Valentine's Day Dance. Frankie Baker, that was her name.

She knelt down in the leaves beside her. "Frankie?" she said softly. "What's wrong? Can I help?"

The girl raised her tear-streaked face. "I'm all right," she gasped. "It's nothing."

Frankie covered her face with her hands and started to sob again.

"It can't be nothing if it makes you feel this bad," Diana said. "Has someone done something to you?"

"N-no," she stammered. "It's my own fault, really."

"What is? Do you feel like talking about it?"

"All I wanted was for him to notice me," Frankie said. She wiped her cheeks on the sleeve of her jacket. "That's not much to ask, is it? But Roxanne's right. I'm just not the kind of girl guys are attracted to."

"That's a ridiculous thing to say," Diana said. "Ridiculous and cruel. There are all kinds of guys out there, and they're attracted to all kinds of girls. I don't really know you, Frankie, but I can see you're pretty and sweet and very bright. All you need is a little more faith in yourself."

Frankie shook her head. "It's nice of you to say that, but it's no use. Why would a guy like Zachary McGraw be interested in me? He just wants me to be his pal and listen to his problems with other girls."

"Zachary?" Diana said carefully. "The football player?"

Frankie nodded. "Uh-huh. I thought after Holly Daniels told him she was in love with somebody else and didn't want anything to do with him, maybe I'd have a chance. But that just made him crazier about her. He even went down to some debate she was in, to show her that he wanted to be friends with her. But Holly didn't want that, either. She told him to go away, and never to speak to her again."

Diana's eyes widened. "She did?"

"Yes," Frankie said. "I'm sorry to go on and on about this, but it really stinks. All Zack can think about is Holly . . . and she doesn't even want him around. I'd never treat him that way, but he doesn't even know I'm alive."

Diana's heart fell. What had she done? And was there enough time to undo it? "Listen, Frankie, I feel horrible about what's happened to you. But you can't stay here like this. Here, wipe your eyes, and come with me. We'll find someone to help cheer you up."

She walked with Frankie out to the meadow,

trying not to let her impatience show; she was grateful to Frankie for straightening this mess out. But she also was losing precious seconds. In one hour, Bart would be on a plane back to Montana, and it would be too late.

Chapter
15

Holly walked slowly down the hill toward the bus stop. Her mother was working late at the dental office this afternoon, so Holly would have the house to herself when she got home. She could use the time to study for her next chemistry test. The letter she'd gotten from the University of Montana had made it very clear that she was expected to keep her grades up through the spring term. It would be nice to finish the year knowing that there was some part of her life she hadn't messed up, she thought.

"Holly! Hey, Holly! Please wait!"

She looked back. Diana was running down the hill after her, waving madly and going so fast that Holly was afraid she would trip and go flying onto her face. After what had happened she couldn't imagine why Diana would be so anxious to talk to her.

Diana skidded to a stop beside her. "Oh," she

said panting and gasping for breath, "I'm so glad I caught you!"

Holly was starting to get alarmed. "What is it? What's wrong?"

"Everything! Me! I just found out how wrong I've been all this time."

"What are you — "

"About everything! About you and Zachary! When I saw him up there hugging you, I was so sure that you'd lied to me. I got so furious that I never even wondered if I might be wrong. But I was, wasn't I?" She gulped. "Oh, Holly, I just know you'll never forgive me! You'll never speak to me again, will you?"

"Of course I will!" Holly opened her arms and gave Diana a hug. Tears of relief dampened her eyes. Was it possible that everything was going to work out after all? That she would regain her best friend *and* her boyfriend, after giving them both up as lost?

"I hoped you'd find out the truth someday," Holly added. "I'm just glad it happened so soon. I don't know if I could have stood it much longer. But you've got to promise me that you'll call Bart the minute you get home and tell him. Better yet, maybe we can call him together."

"But that's just it!" Diana wailed. "I lied to you! I wanted to protect him, so I told you he was going back early, but he wasn't. He's been in Rose Hill all week, just sitting around and sulking. He didn't even go out once with the guys."

"He's still here? He hasn't gone?" Without thinking, she turned to dash down the hill. She might even have tried to run the two or three miles to the Einerson house if Diana's words hadn't stopped her.

"But he's leaving this afternoon," she went on. "He's probably at the airport already. I would have gone to see him off, but I had to work on the festival."

"I've got to catch him!" Holly said in a frantic voice. "What'll I do? I don't have a car."

"I'll drive you," Diana announced. "Come on."

"But what about the festival? You're the organizer. You can't just leave like that!"

"Oh, yes, I can. This whole mess is my fault, and I'm going to do whatever I can to straighten it out. Come on, we're losing time!"

"There's no point," Holly said in a despondent voice. "It's already past three-thirty, and we haven't even found a parking spot."

Diana turned into another row of the airport parking lot. "I'm not quitting until I know that plane is in the air," she replied. "Airline schedules don't mean much these days. They're always delaying flights or canceling them or something. Look — there's someone pulling out!"

Moments later the car was parked, and Holly was breathlessly following her friend across the access road to the terminal. Diana paused just inside the door and studied the departure monitor. "There," she said triumphantly. "Didn't I tell you? His flight's been delayed. Come on!"

They hurried through the building in the direction of Bart's gate, dodging around luggage carts, whole families, and people sitting on their suitcases. Holly's heart was beating faster and faster. What would Bart do? How would he react?

"May I see your tickets, please?"

They skidded to a halt in front of the metal detector. "We're not on a flight," Diana said. "We just need to talk to someone who is."

"I'm sorry," the guard said. "You can't go through." He pointed up at a sign that read: ONLY PASSENGERS HOLDING TICKETS PERMITTED PAST THIS POINT.

"Oh no!" Holly wailed. "I've just *got* to see him!"

It was the worst kind of torture she could imagine. Bart was only two hundred feet away, but he might as well have been in Australia. Any minute now he would get on that plane thinking that Holly didn't love him. And here she was standing just a short distance away from him, hoping for the chance to prove to him that he was the only boy in the world she loved.

Diana took her arm. "Look," she said to the guard, "my brother is leaving on flight forty-five, from gate ten. The flight's been delayed, so I know he's still there. Can't I just go tell him to come out here?"

"Sorry," the guard said. "A rule's a rule."

Shoulders slumping, Holly turned to walk away, but Diana held onto her arm and wouldn't let her go.

"Listen, officer," she continued, "can somebody take a message to him? It's really important."

The guard shrugged. "Well, I guess you could ask the airline to page him. Try over at the service desk."

The two girls raced to the service desk, but there was no one behind it when they got there. Holly looked over her shoulder as if expecting to see Bart's airplane looming through the wide windows of the terminal. Every moment wasted was a moment lost forever.

A woman finally appeared behind the counter. Diana explained what they wanted, and the woman nodded. She picked up a microphone and her voice boomed through the terminal. "Bart Einerson, Bart Einerson, passenger on flight forty-five, please report to the service counter in the central concourse."

Holly stared in the direction of the metal detectors, hoping to see Bart's tall, rugged form, but no one came. The woman waited a little longer, then repeated the announcement. Still no response.

Suddenly, behind her, a familiar voice said, "Excuse me, is this the service counter?"

Holly spun around. Bart saw her and froze with shock. She hated to see the longing and pain in his face, but she didn't dare go to him, not yet. Diana took his arm and pulled him aside. As she spoke, Holly watched the expression on his face change from bafflement to anger to hope. Then he looked over and met her eyes, and she knew everything was finally going to be all right.

An instant later, she was wrapped tight in his arms and they were kissing with all the pent-up emotions of the terrible week they had lost. The embrace went on and on. Finally Holly pulled back and whispered, "I have a surprise for you."

"What?" he said, studying her face.

171

"I was accepted by Montana, with financial aid," she told him. "Once September comes, we won't have to be apart *anymore*. Are you happy?"

"I couldn't be happier. How about you?"

"I'll be sad when you have to catch your plane, but until then, I'm the happiest person in the world!" Over Bart's shoulder, she saw Diana smiling at them. Then his lips met hers once more, and she closed her eyes.

Katie leaned against the office door and took a firmer grip on her cane. She had just spent most of her session with the physical therapist learning how to walk with it. The practice had helped her feel fairly confident physically, but it hadn't improved her general state of mind. It was true that the cane was a lot less cumbersome than crutches, and it called less attention to her disability, but she still resented it. It was proof of the fact that her body had let her down, and if it had let her down once, it could do it again. Katie wondered dully if she could ever again launch herself into a complex and risky routine with the total confidence a winner had to have.

She hesitated as she reached the sidewalk. In spite of their fight, Greg was still expecting her to show up at the Maple Sugarin' Festival. All her friends were bound to be there, too. The bus that stopped just down the block would take her to the Nature Center, though when she got there she would still have a long uphill walk. And once she managed the climb, she would have to walk around the festival, or stand around while everyone talked and joked. Her good leg already ached;

after all that, it would be tied into a tight knot of pain. She couldn't take any more of this — either the physical pain or the pain of knowing she couldn't do any of the fun things her friends would be doing.

The alternative was simple: call her mother and ask her to come pick her up. At home she could lie down and rest, but Katie knew with sick certainty that if she did, she would sink deeper into the despondency that had been threatening to overcome her ever since the accident.

Either way, she would feel terrible. But she felt terrible now anyway. When in doubt, put off a decision, she thought glumly. A month before, she would have had contempt for someone so wimpy, but a lot had changed for her in a month. She walked slowly over to a bench and sat down. In her jacket was the latest issue of *The Red and the Gold*, which she hadn't had time to look at yet. She might as well find out what the rest of the school was up to. She pulled it out and unfolded it.

Holly and Greg had made the front page. Karen's article did a good job of explaining how difficult the invitational tournament had been and how remarkable it was that the Kennedy team had taken third place. The photo showed Greg leaning over the podium, gesturing with his fist. He looked like a winner — very distinguished, very forceful, and very successful.

There was another winner on the front page, too, a girl from Stevenson who had won first place in humorous improv at the tournament.

Not only was she a winner, but according to Karen's interview of her, she was a winner who had overcome almost incredible obstacles.

A blast of sound disrupted Katie's concentration. Three kids had just come out of The Hall of Shame. One of them climbed into a battered Mustang and revved the engine while the other two stood around talking to him over the motor's roar. As she watched, the Mustang peeled out, leaving a stinking cloud of blue smoke behind it. One of the two guys left at the curb noticed her, and said something to the other one. She looked down hastily.

She flipped to the back page of the paper, hoping to distract herself. The headline was about the swim team's successful season, with a photo of her ex-boyfriend Eric, the captain of the team, looking like a real competitor. Another article described the first gymnastics meet of the season. The sensation of the day had been a recent transfer student from Stevenson, sophomore Stacy Morrison. The reporter who'd written the article went on to say that she thought Stacy would soon overshadow Katie Crawford, last season's top-rated gymnast, who was now sidelined after a skiing accident.

Would soon overshadow? Katie sniffed. What about the higher scores she'd achieved at every meet where they'd both competed? But the comment hurt anyway. The reporter was practically telling the world that Katie was past her prime and should make way for the new generation. Past her prime, at seventeen? She studied the picture of Stacy at the conclusion of her floor routine. Her form looked good, all right, but not *really* good. There was something about it that was too showy, not professional enough. Katie tossed the paper onto the bench and stared at the sky. Maybe she was wrong; maybe Stacy really was better than she had been. Had been. *Has-been.* Was that it, was she a has-been already?

It was funny, in a way. All her friends were looking forward to college, and to careers. They had everything in front of them, and they couldn't wait to get going. But she was feeling more and more like the future didn't hold anything for her. Her triumphs were already in the past. Until the accident, she had been going along expecting those triumphs to continue and to lead to bigger, more gratifying victories. But maybe it didn't work that way. After all, most gymnasts peaked in their late teens and were never really able to recapture that form as they got older. Maybe it had just ended a little earlier for her, that was all.

She couldn't face her friends, not now. They were all going to be among the winners, but she was already washed up. And she didn't want to go home, where everyone was so concerned about her. What was the point of that if she wasn't going to have a future to be concerned about? What she really wanted was to be away from everyone, even herself.

Suddenly decisive, she grabbed her cane and struggled to her feet. As she hobbled toward The Hall of Shame, the insistent throb of the music inside the club grew louder and more enveloping. The music had begun growing on her, after all the time she'd spent waiting for rides home from her physical therapy. She tugged the door open and found herself in a dark hallway with tattered photos of punk rock groups tacked to the walls. She groped her way toward a man watching TV at a beat-up table, paid him two dollars for a ticket, then pushed through a thick, dusty curtain into the club.

Three or four colored spotlights lit a small stage where a scruffy-looking band was pounding out loud rock on their instruments. A couple of dozen people were scattered around the room at tables that looked like they had come from a junkyard. No one turned to look at her as she pulled out an initial-carved wooden chair and sat down.

In some way she didn't quite understand, this felt like the place for her. She belonged here. More than that, she liked being here. In this dark, noisy room she could be by herself. No one expected her to be cheerful, or skilled, or a winner. No one expected anything at all of her.

"Hey, girl."

Katie jumped, startled out of her gloomy thoughts. She looked up at the guy next to her. His ragged hair curled over his ears. Over a black T-shirt he wore a grimy denim jacket with ripped-off sleeves. He chuckled.

"Easy, babe. What's got you so wired?"

"Sorry," she said. "I just wasn't expecting anybody to sneak up on me like that."

The guy smiled crookedly. "Don't tell me. This is your first time in here, right?"

Katie nodded.

"Yeah, I thought so. Did your girlfriends dare

you or something? You don't look like the kind of girl who usually hangs out here."

"Oh, no?" Katie said. "Well, you're wrong. Nobody dared me. I came in here because I wanted to. And what makes you think you know anything about the kind of girl I am?"

The guy placed his palms on the table and leaned forward until his face was just a few inches from Katie's. "In that case," he said softly, "maybe I should find out more about you. Mind if I sit down for a while?"

Katie stifled a gasp. Two months earlier, she couldn't have imagined even speaking to a boy like this. Now she felt drawn to him. He'd been through *something*, she could see that in his big, sad eyes — something as awful as what she was going through. He could understand her in a way that her friends — her former friends, her winner friends with their perfect lives — never would.

"Sure," she said, sliding her chair over. "Sit down. I'm not going anywhere in a hurry."

Coming soon . . .
Couples #30
FALLING FOR YOU

Frankie thought she would never stop laughing. Hand in hand, she and Josh raced across the Commons after their secret mission was accomplished.

"WEEE DID IT! WAHOOOO!" Frankie hollered.

"YEEEE-HAA!" Josh bellowed. "Good work, *Hildy Muldoon!*" he cheered, calling Frankie by her alias. Josh jumped high into the air and tried as hard as he could to click his heels.

Frankie pulled Josh across the lawn, practically making him fall on his face. Josh caught up and grabbed her other arm. Together they swung each other around in a circle, bursting with joy. At first Frankie was aware of the curious stares from the people around her, then she saw only a blur as they went faster . . . faster. . . .

Before she knew it, they were on the ground, dissolving into dizzy, giddy laughter. But when Frankie looked over at Josh, she realized she was staring into the handsomest face she had ever seen.

Frankie rolled closer to him, her mind reeling and her chest pounding from so much laughter. Josh rolled, too, and suddenly they were eye-to-eye. The silence was electric. Before Frankie could think about what was happening, she and Josh were wrapped in each other's arms. His passionate smile was the last thing she saw before her eyes closed in a tender, hcart-stopping kiss.

She felt as if the two of them were suspended in outer space, on a planet all their own, just floating forever. She didn't want their lips to part. She wanted to stay like this forever, remembering how every inch of her body felt, memorizing every tingle that shot through her.

When they finally, gently pulled apart, they still held each other. Frankie sighed and buried her face in his chest. The whole world could have been watching them and she wouldn't have cared.

Don't miss any exciting adventures of the popular Cheerleaders of Tarenton High!

Complete series available wherever you buy books.

SUNFIRE®

Read all about the fascinating young women who lived and loved during America's most turbulent times!

☐ 32774-7		**AMANDA** Candice F. Ransom	**$2.95**
☐ 33064-0		**SUSANNAH** Candice F. Ransom	**$2.95**
☐ 33156-6		**DANIELLE** Vivian Schurfranz	**$2.95**
☐ 33241-4	#5	**JOANNA** Jane Claypool Miner	**$2.95**
☐ 33242-2	#6	**JESSICA** Mary Francis Shura	**$2.95**
☐ 33239-2	#7	**CAROLINE** Willo Davis Roberts	**$2.95**
☐ 33688-6	#14	**CASSIE** Vivian Schurfranz	**$2.95**
☐ 33686-X	#15	**ROXANNE** Jane Claypool Miner	**$2.95**
☐ 41468-2	#16	**MEGAN** Vivian Schurfranz	**$2.75**
☐ 41438-0	#17	**SABRINA** Candice F. Ransom	**$2.75**
☐ 33933-8	#18	**VERONICA** Jane Claypool Miner	**$2.25**
☐ 40049-5	#19	**NICOLE** Candice F. Ransom	**$2.25**
☐ 40268-4	#20	**JULIE** Vivian Schurfranz	**$2.25**
☐ 40394-X	#21	**RACHEL** Vivian Schurfranz	**$2.50**
☐ 40395-8	#22	**COREY** Jane Claypool Miner	**$2.50**
☐ 40717-1	#23	**HEATHER** Vivian Schurfranz	**$2.50**
☐ 40716-3	#24	**GABRIELLE** Mary Francis Shura	**$2.50**
☐ 41000-8	#25	**MERRIE** Vivian Schurfranz	**$2.75**
☐ 41012-1	#26	**NORA** Jeffie Ross Gordon	**$2.75**
☐ 41191-8	#27	**MARGARET** Jane Claypool Miner	**$2.75**

Complete series available wherever you buy books.

Scholastic Inc.
P.O. Box 7502, 2932 East McCarty Street, Jefferson City, MO 65102

Please send me the books I have checked above. I am enclosing $_____
(please add $1.00 to cover shipping and handling). Send check or money order—no cash or C.O.D.'s please.

Name_____

Address_____

City_____State/Zip_____

Please allow four to six weeks for delivery. Offer good in U.S.A. only. Sorry, mail order not available to residents of Canada. Prices subject to change.

SUN987